RED GUARD FANTASIES
and
Other Stories

Shouhua Qi

LONG RIVER PRESS
San Francisco

Published in the United States of America by

Long River Press
360 Swift Avenue, #48
South San Francisco, CA 94080
www.longriverpress.com

Editor: Chris Robyn
Designer: Tommy Liu
Cover illustration: Ken Cox

ISBN-10: 1-59265-068-6
ISBN-13: 978-1-59265-068-2

First Edition 2007

Printed in China

10 9 8 7 6 5 4 3 2 1

"The Evidence" was originally published in *Feminist Studies*, Volume 31, Number 3 (Summer 2005): 400-415, by permission of the publisher, Feminist Studies, Inc.

"Red Guard's Fantasies" and "Love Me, Love My Dog" were first published in the quarterly UK arts journal, *Ambit*, issues 181 (2005), and 184 (2006), respectively.

Library of Congress Cataloging-in-Publication Data

Qi, Shouhua.
Red Guard fantasies and other stories / Shouhua Qi.-- 1st ed.
p. cm.
ISBN 1-59265-068-6
1. China--History--1976-2002--Fiction. 2. Popular culture--China--History--20th century--Fiction. I. Title.
PS3617.I15R43 2006
813'.6--dc22

2006004097

For my father

Contents

Author's Note

I was once a Red Guard. Sort of.

When the Great Proletariat Cultural Revolution (1966-1976) started, I was nine years old and my father, the principal of a middle school outside the city walls of Nanjing, got into serious trouble with a handful of disgruntled teachers and unruly pupils who were now given a cause to rebel for. I was to witness my father being forced to kneel on shards of broken glass with a heavy wood-framed chalkboard—a sick twist on the cangue once used in old China—hanging from his neck. I also watched him suffer other indignities during numerous loud denunciation rallies and so-called "struggle sessions," in which the poor recipient is accused and then shouted down by an angry mob: all too common in those days.

I didn't have the privilege to wear a Red Guard band on my arm until my first year in middle school when my father was semi-"liberated" from his alleged crimes against the Party. By then, it was too late for me to catch the train that had carried a generation of boisterous youths all over the country to smash all things old, bourgeois, and feudalistic, and to spread the prairie fire of Revolution, a fire which had all but burned the life out of a five-thousand-year-old civilization.

Father refused to be crushed. He picked himself up and forged ahead, his head high, his faith unwavering, his passionate devotion to education of the underprivileged not a bit diminished.

The stories collected here are "fantasies" of a former Red Guard. They are about people caught in the unsettling dramas of Chinese society accelerating at a blistering pace in the decades after the Cultural Revolution.

The Evidence

When the two uniformed Public Security officers walked in, Fangmei was more annoyed than scared. Cheapskates. The last time they came, after being fussed over for an hour, they didn't pay a cent.

"Just a sec," she said to the officers, brushing more shaving cream on the sideburns of a client reclining deliciously in the chair. "I'll be done with this gentleman in no time."

It was the shorter of the two officers, who had six or seven long hairs curling up at the tip of his chin and didn't want her to shave them, who had fumbled with his leather wallet before leaving. "Didn't bring any money with me today. Pay you next time. Okay?"

The taller one didn't even bother. She remembered being nettled by the bold gleam from his protruding pupils wandering knowingly on her face when she bent closer to trim those long, thick, wettish hairs sticking out of his garlic-shaped nose. He had very bad breath, too.

Being a hairdresser hadn't exactly been Fangmei's girlish dream. She wasn't the prettiest among her classmates, yet a luster of dreaminess—of an indefinable longing, toned by a faint, almost sad pensiveness—would surface from the depth of her almond-shaped eyes when she was not on guard. Conscious of being noticed, the dreamy expression would vanish with one blink of her long eyelashes. However, she didn't do well enough to impress any college or university admission officials; none of her classmates in the rural school did anyway.

"What will you do?" Pa had said over supper (cornmeal cakes and smoked pork mixed with green onion) on the night of her graduation. "Help me raise pigs?"

"Going to be a hairdresser at Shanhe Town," she announced, nonchalantly.

"Crazy girl." What he really wanted to say was that he felt uneasy about letting his only daughter mess with people's hair—especially men's hair—for a living, but he didn't want her to be stuck on the small ten-*mu* farm forever, either.

He didn't say another word. He knew his daughter and there was no use trying to change her mind. Shanhe Town was only a few hours' ride away—by tractor. At least it would be better than going by train night and day to faraway places and working as a live-in maid in some rich person's home, like a few of her friends were planning to do. He had heard the rumors.

"No, we're not here for haircuts," the short officer finally said, flatly, sticking out his sparsely-haired chin.

"Huh? Not here for haircuts?" Fangmei gave a quick glance at the officers, her left thumb resting on the edge of the sideburns of her client; her right hand holding the sharp, long-bladed razor moving rhythmically, leaving a clean track like a snow shovel.

"Miss, you're under arrest," the tall officer growled hoarsely. Fangmei could smell the odor of cheap cigarettes and strong liquor come out of his mouth and flood into the room.

"Arrest? Me?" Fangmei was stunned, wide-eyed. Her right hand was frozen in midair, her mouth agape, the blood rushing to her cheeks. "What did I do?" She turned to face the officers.

"You'll find out. Now come with us," the tall officer urged once more.

"I—" Fangmei stammered; she felt the razor slip out of her hand and land with a clink on the floor.

"Don't waste our time with any nonsense," growled the tall officer, both to Fangmei and to the middle-aged patron, who had already sat up from the chair, looking worried, half of his face still covered in a thick layer of shaving cream. The officer stepped closer and put handcuffs around Fangmei's trembling wrists. They ratcheted shut with a click.

"Oww!" Fangmei let out a cry. Something warm was welling up in her eyes. No tears. No tears, no matter what. She remembered crying herself to sleep on a wintry night many years ago when she realized that Ma had left and would never come home. She'd never allowed herself to shed another tear since then, not even when being chased by naughty kids calling her names.

The middle-aged man wriggled his way out of the chair and hurried out the door. An elderly man and a matronly woman, who had been sitting on a bench near the door, waiting for their turn, also got up quietly and shuffled out.

When the police vehicle, a white Toyota minivan with rusty spots near the door handle, started to move, she turned to glance at the "Fangmei Hairdresser's" sign she had made with a piece of wooden board painted white.

All the trouble she had gone through to get started: apprenticing for months without being paid a cent; Pa selling half a dozen of the almost-fattened pigs for her to rent this small bare brick and cement space; buying clippers, combs, razors, a blow-dryer; the creamy white and sky-blue paint dripping all over her hair, face, and clothes while she fixed up and decorated the place. . . it all just ended like this? She could still see that timid girl standing under "Fangmei Hairdresser's," greeting prospective customers: "Want a haircut?"

"If you haven't done anything shameful," she murmured over and over in the back of the van, "you shouldn't be scared of ghosts knocking on your door at midnight." Somehow, though, she *was* scared.

The short officer was driving. The tall officer was squeezed in next to her in the back seat. He breathed heavily. Fangmei turned her face toward the window. She cringed when she felt his right leg touching—rubbing, in fact—hers, as the van bumped ahead along the rutted street. The muscles in his leg were tensed and eager. His legs must be hairy, too. She was disgusted by the thought and was annoyed with herself for having thought it. She moved herself closer to the side of the van, huddled protectively against the window, and turning her entire body away from him to look outside. The tall officer's garlic-shaped nose grunted and she could feel his burning stare against the nape of her neck. There was no place to hide.

The mid-autumn sky of Shanhe Town was enveloped in a drowsy, grayish mist. It was early afternoon. Along the narrow lanes was an old bicycle repair shop, the racks on its walls being draped with used tires, tubes, wheels, and handlebars; next to that was a seamstress' with newly-made khaki pants and floral-patterned women's clothes hanging in a dusty window; a recycling store, its door half-blocked by bundles of yellowed newspapers and neatly-flattened cardboard boxes; a low, sorry-looking two-story residence, its almost-bare wooden door and window frames betraying the benefit of fresh red paint in its more prosperous days.

As the van neared the town square, the street became wider, smoother, and the traffic heavier. There were sputtering, buzzing motorcycles, rumbling trucks, slow, groaning tractors, and a couple of screechy long-distance buses covered in dust. A shiny, beige Volkswagen sedan and a blue Chevrolet van were caught in the same current and drifted along uneasily. The air suddenly grew thick and dirty.

How many bottles of shampoo would it take to wash it all clean?

Now on display in the store windows were colorful dresses, TVs of every size, CDs, and videos. There were shops selling ceramic tile, wallpaper, and other building materials. Throaty, unintelligible cooing of pop stars; the frenzied howling of a Liu Huang, as if stranded in the wilderness of the Gobi desert, and impassioned revolutionary hymns from a long, bygone era, were blasted out to the street from inside the music stores, fading in and out as the police van honked its way ahead.

Before the van turned into a side street, she caught a glimpse of a huge scarlet banner on top of a tall, half-finished building; the huge characters in the banner grandly proclaiming something about transforming Shanhe Town into a first-rate twenty-first-century city.

One day, she had told herself the last time she had happened to pass the town square, she would set up a real beauty salon here. She would have large, full-length mirrors, black-and-white tile floor, and use nothing but the best, imported shampoo, conditioner, styling refresher, shaping gel, and foaming pomade. In the spotless glass display window which faced the busy street, she would display framed pictures of the most glamorous hairstyles she could design. She would hire a few good girls like herself, and train them well.

What would that matter now? She sighed.

Her life had been suspended.

Disrupted.

She was a criminal sitting handcuffed in a police van. But what crime had she committed?

She turned her eyes away from the window to huddled lower in the seat. She didn't want any passers-by to see her face.

The van jerked to a stop. Fangmei looked outside. It had parked inside a small, walled compound. After the short officer slid open the door, Fangmei eased herself out of the van.

On her right was a small vineyard; clusters of small, emerald-colored, sour-looking grapes were peeping out of dark-green leaves and creeping vines supported by a rusty metal frame. On her left was a bicycle shed with grass-green corrugated fiberglass top covered with patches of dirty moss and a few brown leaves. Next to the shed were parked a brand new chartreuse Beijing Jeep and another white Toyota van, both sparkling clean.

She was led inside the building, through a short hallway with offices on both sides, and into the "Interrogation Room" at the end.

There was an old brown writing desk at the deep end of the room, three chairs behind the desk, and another chair—its paint having chipped off—placed right in the middle of the room. She took a few steps into the room. They led her to the chair where she stood for a moment behind it.

"Chief, we've got the criminal," she heard the short officer reporting somewhere in the hallway.

Muffled voices.

A pause.

She heard footsteps coming to the Interrogation Room. They were not hurried, but slow and methodical.

The chief walked into the room and sat down behind the desk in the middle of the three chairs.

He was stout, middle-aged, ruddy, somewhat lumpy, the flesh around the square jaw hanging a bit lazily. He had a full head of hair, though the top had begun to thin; it was combed all the way back, neat, puffed up, a benefit of generous use of mousse and hairspray. The sharply-creased grass-green wool uniform gave him an authoritative, almost distinguished air.

The chief picked up a burgundy folder from the desk, tapped at it a few times, and looked up to fix his gaze on Fangmei. The tall and short officers had already positioned themselves, one on each side of the desk.

He paused, as if to give Fangmei enough time to appreciate the weight of the slogans posted on the walls, written in thick, dark ink, and bold, masculine brushstrokes:

Cracking Down on Crimes
Protecting Social Stability

Leniency to Those Who Confess and Cooperate
Harshness to Those Who Choose to Resist

"Un-cuff the criminal," the chief said, in a measured tone. His voice was thin, somewhat shrill, like when you wiped a mirror with window cleaner a bit too hard.

The tall officer marched over from behind the desk, fumbled with his keys, and unlocked the handcuffs.

"Now, take a seat," the chief nodded to the chair in the center of the room.

Maybe he would understand. He seemed different from the other two.

"I—" Fangmei wanted to explain that it was all a mistake, but was choked by something warm rushing up from her chest, all the way to her eyelids. No. She swallowed it down.

"Your name?" the chief asked.

"Wu Fangmei." She saw the short officer taking notes.

"Age?"

"20."

"Original residence?"

"Wu Village, Anyan County."

"Profession?"

"Hairdresser."

A pause.

"Now, Miss Wu," the chief said, taking out a cigarette box, fishing one out. He was about to light it when the short officer's hand rushed up and flicked on his lighter.

"You know why we've arrested you today?" It was more of a statement than a question.

"No."

"You don't know?" The chief sounded both incredulous and disappointed. He took a long drag on the cigarette and spat out a string of bluish rings into the air. "You look like an intelligent young woman and should know our policies."

"Yes, I do, but—" Fangmei mumbled.

"Then confess and cooperate."

"I. . .I don't know what. . .what to confess. Honestly."

"Now, let me remind you of something. What do you do for a living?"

"Hairdresser."

"Hairdresser?" The same measured tone, but the way the chief repeated the word, as if that was not the expected answer, as if something not quite right was associated with it, made Fangmei's heart skip a beat.

"Come on, Miss Wu. You know that I know what's going on in Shanhe Town. You and I know what kind of services are available behind the closed doors of hairdresser shops, beauty salons, and massage parlors." He paused, taking another drag on the cigarette. "Look, although our policies are to encourage enterprising people to get rich first, well, that doesn't mean that you can. . ." He paused.

"It doesn't mean you can sneak your way into folks' wallets by dropping your pants!" the tall officer finished the sentence, matter-of-factly.

The chief waved for him to be quiet.

"Think. Think hard," the chief said patiently. "Everything depends on your attitude."

Behind closed doors? After cleaning up, she would watch a bit of TV, her favorite pastime, over supper. *Love Connections, Holding Hands, For Whom Does Your Heart Beat?* Those were her favorites. Watching fashionably dressed young men and women pouring out their hearts and picking out dates in front of millions of TV viewers. She would smile, sigh, and shake her head incredulously at the contestants. People in big cities really knew how to have fun. Her eyes would be riveted on the hair styles of people in those shows, critiquing this and admiring that. Occasionally, CCTV ran footage of fashion shows held in Hong Kong, Paris, and even Guangzhou.

Once, spurred on by a sudden urge while watching tall, slinky supermodels swinging their hips down the runway and showing lots of cleavage, she jumped out of the chair, walked back and forth quite a few times in the shop, thrusting her hips this way and that way, awkwardly. She felt the blood rushing to her face and her heart pounding audibly while doing so.

"Bad girl," she pointed an imaginary finger at her own little nose and hurried back to the chair, her face still hot to the earlobes.

Another favorite pastime was to play with her long, shiny, waist-length hair. She'd fix it up, down, half up and half down, let it cascade down her chest or fall rippling behind her back. One style she liked the most was the pleat: holding the hair of the upper part of her head, winding it, counterclockwise, then folding it many times towards the right side, and fixing it at the rear of her head with hair pins, in a nice roll; then gathering the hair of the lower part of her head, winding it in the opposite direction of the upper part. She'd be amazed by how elegant the girl in the mirror looked.

When it got really late, she'd sit in bed, leafing through the dog-eared pages of old fashion magazines bought at roadside stands, until she fell asleep.

"Now, have you thought it through?" the chief coughed. The thin, scratchy voice aroused her from the reverie.

"Yes, but I couldn't find anything. . . anything criminal

that I've done."

A pause.

"Why did you close your door last Tuesday, during business hours? At around two in the afternoon?" the chief said, measuredly.

"Last Tuesday? Around two? Oh! I went to the Electricity Bureau to pay the bill."

"Any witnesses?"

"No . . .But, you can check with the Electricity Bureau."

"You don't think we know what's going on?"

"Two weeks ago," the tall officer cut in, "I saw a man entering the shop. Then, I saw you closing the door."

"What? I never close the door during business hours. Oh . . . now I remember!. . . It has to be the day of the sandstorm. Remember the sandstorm? Brown dust as thick as fog? I had to close the door that day when the storm hit."

Another short pause.

"One Saturday evening last month," the chief said, deliberately, as if reading from the folder, "at around 8:30pm, a man entered the shop. He didn't leave until six o'clock the next morning."

"That . . .that was my Pa! He came to see how I was doing."

"Okay, Miss Wu, you seem to have a ready answer for everything." The chief's tone was still measured. "Your attitude is really, really bad."

"I'll help her find the right attitude," the tall officer said. He walked right up to Fangmei, grabbed the collar of her thin white blouse with his knurled hand, and slapped her in quick succession on both cheeks, right and left. "You little bitch! Think you'd pull the wool over our eyes?"

Blinded, she felt an icy numbness in her cheeks, as if they'd suddenly been sliced right off her face.

The chief sat back in his chair and sighed. The short officer gazed at her, motionless.

"See, you've got to cooperate," the chief said, helplessly, "otherwise, I cannot protect you."

"Tell . . .tell . . .me . . .how . . .to . . . ," Fangmei struggled to hold back the tears.

"Tell us who are your . . .'patrons'," the chief drew out the word deliberately. He picked up the burgundy folder, tapped at it once, his gaze all the time fixed on Fangmei's face. "*They've* all confessed, you know? I just want to give you a chance. It all depends on your attitude."

The detention room was about ten feet square and bare, with gray brick walks and a cold cement floor. There was a narrow, barred window with an opaque cover high up on the wall almost against the ceiling. It let in a feeble cast of light from somewhere outside. The air was still and damp and smelled of urine. She huddled down in a corner, gingerly. The wet, sticky cement floor sent chills up her spine and caused her temples to throb.

No amount of shampoo would wash this place clean.

She sat, staring blankly, for hours, until the faint light from the barred window had long faded to black.

It was all like a bad dream. How did it all start? From the time Ma left? She had never figured out why. Pa never wanted to talk about it. She had overheard folks gossiping about Ma running away with an itinerant carpenter. For love? Or for a chance to get out of stark poverty? Nobody knew. She knew vaguely that running away with a man was bad. She had nursed that shame in her heart and vowed she'd never do anything shameful.

Had she done anything shameful as a hairdresser? Anything criminal? No. She felt she had a clear record and a clearer conscience. She had made sure she paid her rent and all the bills on time. Even when the town tax-collecting officials threw outrageous bills at her, she didn't complain. She knew it was all part of doing business. Yes, most of her customers were men. She vaguely knew the reasons why, but the way she conducted herself with them should not have given anyone the wrong idea.

Men had made passes at her:

"Aren't you afraid at night? Need someone to keep you company?"

Some—she could see their reflections in the mirror on the wall—would let their eyes roam hungrily on her face, her chest, just as the tall officer had, when she was in the middle of clipping or trimming their hair.

She'd be nettled, but pretend not to hear or notice.

One late afternoon, the owner of a small karaoke hall down the street, a fiftyish, balding man, gripped her hand when paying for the haircut and tried to pull her toward him. She was so frightened.

"Get out!" she screamed, after breaking free from his hand. He rushed out.

He never came back.

There was one time, though, only one time, when she may have let her guard down. She blushed profusely.

It was before closing time one early August evening. Lulu, a regular, came for a haircut. He was in his late twenties, not very tall, but well-built, and had an open expression on his face. He was a chef at a small Sichuan restaurant a few streets from Fangmei Hairdresser's. Sitting in the chair, while Fangmei worked on his hair, he'd carry on small talk with her. More exactly, he talked and Fangmei responded with affirmative "uh-huhs." Fangmei got to know how he disliked the miserly restaurant owner and how he didn't want to waste money on drinks and cigarettes so that he'd save up enough money and one day have a restaurant of his own. She didn't know exactly how she should feel about the young man. There was certain empathy there, though. They were both working people, searching for an independent future.

It was that evening, after the haircut, that Lulu asked Fangmei to give him a massage.

"The long hours in the hot kitchen are killing my back," he said.

"No, I. . .I don't know how," Fangmei was taken aback.

"I'll show you," he made Fangmei sit down on a stool. "Sit up, relax your muscles, and breathe easily," Lulu instructed, expertly. There was a nervous excitement in his voice. She wasn't sure this was the right thing to do, but. . . .

When his strong hands rested on her shoulders, she shuddered. His hands began to move, slowly. She didn't know what to feel. She was tense, uncertain. Gentle strokes down her spine. . . muscles being grabbed and lifted lightly. . .his thumbs and fingertips working in deep circles. . . gentle chopping, beating, and tapping. . . more strokes down the spine. . . muscles being grabbed and lifted lightly. . . she wanted to let go, let go of all the soreness that had been deposited deep in the joints and deep in the muscles. . . she wanted to cry. . . she almost let out a moan. . . .

"Stop!" she stood up, abruptly, as if awakening from a dream. "Please go."

Lulu stood there, his hands frozen in air where Fangmei's back had been, as if struck by lightning. A big "Why?" was written all over his face.

"Please just go," she said firmly.

She didn't watch any TV that night. She just sat in the chair, blank, for a long time.

She lost another of her regulars. Someone she almost liked.

The detention room was about ten feet square and bare, with gray brick walls and a cold cement floor. There was a narrow, barred window with an opaque cover high up on the wall almost against the ceiling. It let in a feeble cast of light from somewhere outside. The air was still and damp and smelled of urine. She huddled down in a corner, gingerly. The wet, sticky cement floor sent chills up her spine and caused her temples to throb.

No amount of shampoo would wash this place clean.

She sat, staring blankly, for hours, until the faint light from the barred window had long faded to black.

It was all like a bad dream. How did it all start? From the time Ma left? She had never figured out why. Pa never wanted to talk about it. She had overheard folks gossiping about Ma running away with an itinerant carpenter. For love? Or for a chance to get out of stark poverty? Nobody knew. She knew vaguely that running away with a man was bad. She had nursed that shame in her heart and vowed she'd never do anything shameful.

Had she done anything shameful as a hairdresser? Anything criminal? No. She felt she had a clear record and a clearer conscience. She had made sure she paid her rent and all the bills on time. Even when the town tax-collecting officials threw outrageous bills at her, she didn't complain. She knew it was all part of doing business. Yes, most of her customers were men. She vaguely knew the reasons why, but the way she conducted herself with them should not have given anyone the wrong idea.

Men had made passes at her:

"Aren't you afraid at night? Need someone to keep you company?"

Some—she could see their reflections in the mirror on the wall—would let their eyes roam hungrily on her face, her chest, just as the tall officer had, when she was in the middle of clipping or trimming their hair.

She'd be nettled, but pretend not to hear or notice.

One late afternoon, the owner of a small karaoke hall down the street, a fiftyish, balding man, gripped her hand when paying for the haircut and tried to pull her toward him. She was so frightened.

"Get out!" she screamed, after breaking free from his hand. He rushed out.

He never came back.

There was one time, though, only one time, when she may have let her guard down. She blushed profusely.

It was before closing time one early August evening. Lulu, a regular, came for a haircut. He was in his late twenties, not very tall, but well-built, and had an open expression on his face. He was a chef at a small Sichuan restaurant a few streets from Fangmei Hairdresser's. Sitting in the chair, while Fangmei worked on his hair, he'd carry on small talk with her. More exactly, he talked and Fangmei responded with affirmative "uh-huhs." Fangmei got to know how he disliked the miserly restaurant owner and how he didn't want to waste money on drinks and cigarettes so that he'd save up enough money and one day have a restaurant of his own. She didn't know exactly how she should feel about the young man. There was certain empathy there, though. They were both working people, searching for an independent future.

It was that evening, after the haircut, that Lulu asked Fangmei to give him a massage.

"The long hours in the hot kitchen are killing my back," he said.

"No, I. . . I don't know how," Fangmei was taken aback.

"I'll show you," he made Fangmei sit down on a stool. "Sit up, relax your muscles, and breathe easily," Lulu instructed, expertly. There was a nervous excitement in his voice. She wasn't sure this was the right thing to do, but. . . .

When his strong hands rested on her shoulders, she shuddered. His hands began to move, slowly. She didn't know what to feel. She was tense, uncertain. Gentle strokes down her spine. . . muscles being grabbed and lifted lightly. . . his thumbs and fingertips working in deep circles. . . gentle chopping, beating, and tapping. . . more strokes down the spine. . . muscles being grabbed and lifted lightly. . . she wanted to let go, let go of all the soreness that had been deposited deep in the joints and deep in the muscles. . . she wanted to cry. . . she almost let out a moan. . . .

"Stop!" she stood up, abruptly, as if awakening from a dream. "Please go."

Lulu stood there, his hands frozen in air where Fangmei's back had been, as if struck by lightning. A big "Why?" was written all over his face.

"Please just go," she said firmly.

She didn't watch any TV that night. She just sat in the chair, blank, for a long time.

She lost another of her regulars. Someone she almost liked.

Fangmei didn't remember how she had left the public security station and dragged herself back to her shop; how she had found the small bundle of cash—3,500 *yuan*—hidden in a bottle under the bed, money for Pa to buy fertilizer, new seeds for next spring, and pig feed; how she had dragged herself back to the station to pay the fines—she didn't remember getting a receipt, either; nor how the old tractor driver had allowed her to hitch a ride back to Wu Village.

She had been in bed for days now, refusing to say a word. No tears, either.

Pa stood by her door. He hated himself for having allowed his daughter to go to Shanhe Town to be a hairdresser.

Later, he heard from village folks who had read the County Express that the public security station there had busted a prostitution ring, involving a hairdresser, a karaoke hall owner, a Sichuan restaurant chef, and five or six others. They had all confessed, paid very heavy fines, and been released.

"Did you. . .?" Pa asked, tears welled in his eyes.

"No," Fangmei said, weakly.

Two days later, he saw Fangmei getting up, putting on her best clothes.

"I'm going to sue them," she muttered.

"Crazy girl," he wanted to say, but didn't have the heart to do so. Yes, sue those damn sons of turtles. He had heard people talking about how average folks had sued corrupt government officials and won.

Pa sold the other half dozen of the fattened pigs. They went to Anyan County.

"The evidence against you is solid, undisputable," concluded the Deputy Chief of the county's People's Procuratorate, a man in his late forties. Glancing at the file on his desk, he continued, "You yourself have confessed, signed a document, and paid the fines. So have all your patrons." His voice was even and he looked dignified in his deep-blue uniform and the big-brimmed cap. "If you sue those police officers for illegal arrest, assault, kidnapping, and wrongful imprisonment—without solid evidence—you'd be charged with libel and could end up in jail for a long, long time. Think carefully."

The attorney she had hired looked helpless. Without solid evidence, she could not have justice.

She and Pa left the People's Procuratorate. She wandered aimlessly, listlessly, from street to street. Pa followed.

Hours later, she stopped at a billboard promoting a new line of shampoo and conditioner. The girl in the advertisement had long, wavy hair and the look in her maidenly eyes was so innocent, so pure. Fangmei gazed at that girl for a long time, as if lost.

All of a sudden, she turned around, walked on again, at a much faster, more purposeful pace, stopped to ask the woman behind a magazine stand something. The woman pointed and gestured. Fangmei walked again, almost ran. Pa followed, puzzled.

Inside the compound of Anyan County People's Hospital, patients were trudging around slowly, helped by family or friends, nurses in white gowns hustling here and there quietly, lines of people waiting to pay bills or have their prescriptions filled.

Fangmei ran into the main building, ran through crowds outside doctors' offices on both sides of the hallway: old peasants dozing off on long benches, young couples holding hands, women trying to quiet crying babies. She saw a motherly-looking doctor, standing in front of a crowd of waiting patients. Elbowing her way through the crowd blocking the door of the office, Fangmei dropped to her knees and prostrated herself at the doctor's feet.

"Doctor, please save me! Save me!" she begged, gasping for air.

"Please get up," the doctor said, kindly. "Tell me what's going on here?"

"I won't get up until. . . . until you agree to save me!" Fangmei said, her hands still clutching the doctor's feet, her forehead touching the tips of her shoes.

"How?"

As she was lying there, pants down, waiting to be examined, Fangmei suddenly became nervous.

She suddenly remembered something. In her eagerness to learn to do the splits during gym class, she had pushed her legs a bit too hard and hurt herself. Before going to bed that evening, she saw a few red spots on the inside of her underwear.

That morning in the detention room: did that turtle's son

with a garlic nose have his way before she woke up?

What if? She felt stupid and hated herself for feeling so. No time to turn back now. She already began to feel the doctor's cool fingers touching her.

"You're still a virgin," the doctor announced, as if from another world, through the white gauze mask on her face.

Fangmei lay there.

Motionless.

Silent.

Tears surged up from her heart and flooded her eyes, as if the dyke of the Yellow River had burst, cascaded down her cheeks, and fell, like pearls, onto the pillow.

She wept, shamelessly.

One morning two months later, Fangmei was feeding Pa's dozen young piglets in a fenced sty. A faint smile appeared on her face as she watched the piglets attacking the feed in the stone troughs, noisily, making grunting noises at each other as they crowded in.

Her eyes still had that luster of dreaminess, but they were toned by a heavier, more visible pensiveness. Now and then, she would catch herself staring at things, long and blank.

The piglets' hair, black or white, was smooth and shiny. The belly of the smallest piglet, however, showed signs of ticks: clusters of hair stuck together. She could even see white, sesame-seed shaped baby ticks hidden in the hair.

After the piglets finished their meal, Fangmei tiptoed closer to the smallest pig. Slowly, she reached out her hand, scratched its belly, tentatively, gently. The piglet stood there, its eyes gazing ahead dreamily. Then, it kneeled down, fell on its side, stretched out its little legs, and gave itself completely to Fangmei. It grunted, appreciatively, its skin twitched as Fangmei smoothened its hair with an old, fine-toothed wooden comb to rid its belly of all the ticks.

In the face of solid, undisputable evidence, the county's People's Court had exonerated Fangmei and all of her so-called "patrons," and had ordered 85 *yuan* to be paid to her in restitution, but was still examining her suit against the three police officers.

The Tenants

When she heard the honk from the road behind the house, she knew they had finally arrived. She opened the door and squinted in the shimmering rays of the late afternoon sun sieved through the dozen persimmon trees in the yard.

There it was, outside the low, neatly trimmed evergreen bushes. Cranberry red. No huge, puffy, fresh red silk flower draping its hood. No "Double Happiness" on the windshield. No ornament whatsoever on the car. Just the joy that could overflow the small, quiet Twin-Sun River glimmering along the narrow cinder country road.

Dawei—"Means David in English," the young man had explained, in his low-pitched voice, when he came to check out the place—got out of the car first. Tall, with an abundance of hair gelled and casually parted in the middle, a big smile on his youthful, boyish face. Half a head taller than Shan, perhaps.

Nutrition. Nutrition. When four or five years old, Shan had always offered to clean the dishes at the end of the supper—thin corn porridge mixed with pungent carrot leaves, his trick to get to lick clean whatever was left in everybody else's bowl and the pot, only that everybody else had done a darn good job already.

"Mama Yao, here we are!" Dawei shouted, when he saw her

coming out of the gate, an opening in the bushy fence. He came forward, hair bouncing, shook her hands warmly, turned around, opened the door for the backseat. A girl stepped out.

"My girlfriend, Maliya." Dawei's voice was ringing with pride. "Maria in English."

"Mama Yao," Maliya said softly, reaching out to shake hands.

Slender, cool, supple hand in Mama Yao's sinew-swelled hand which still had the calluses that had been there for many years. Almost a full head shorter than Dawei, hair rippling halfway to the shoulders, silky, lustrous, a wavy tress dangling playfully above the eyebrows. Not exactly a looker. Nothing striking about her eyes, her nose, or her mouth, but they were neatly, pleasantly put together. A low cut—but not revealing—light yellow t-shirt, a thin gold necklace with a small heart-shaped ruby stone resting quietly on her pale skin—a gift from Dawei, perhaps? Faded jean shorts, way above her knees, hugging her girlish hips tightly.

Mama Yao's eyes were all smiles.

The taxi driver had already popped the trunk open. Dawei lifted out a heavy sea blue canvas bag, a smaller, rosy red leather suitcase, a few brownish cardboard boxes, and two bundles of books.

"No, Mama Yao, how can we let you—" Maliya hurried over to stop Mama Yao when she reached for the suitcase. "Dawei can handle it all by himself, right?" Mama Yao could hear the mischievous winking in her clear, flute-like voice.

"Can I?" Dawei sounded skeptical. He grabbed the bag and the suitcase, one in each hand, lifted them, at least a foot above the ground. "Oh, they're going to crush me into the ground," he wailed, gasping for air, his back bending, like a hunchback, ready to drop, then, suddenly, as if hit by a powerful current, his back straightened, his chest puffed out, and he marched toward the house with as much ease as he could muster.

"Naughty!" Maliya giggled, picking up a gourd-shaped case and a couple of other smaller boxes and followed.

Mama Yao trailed behind on the little brick path, carrying two bundles of books.

The book on the top of one bundle had a line of skinny, flowery bean sprouts on the cover—musical notes, of course.

The book on the top of the other bundle had on its cover a few tall, bold-faced foreign—English?—words strung together, hands and legs flying in all directions. They were marching forward, their backs tilted so much to the right as if they were ready to crash at any time.

She caught up with the young couple and unlocked the door next to her own.

The "apartment" had two rooms, furnished: a bedroom and a kitchen-dining-bath room.

The kitchen had a free-standing, two-burner gas stove; its propane tank still more than three quarters full, a small water-heater also hooked to the tank, the water-heater being connected through a thin copper pipe to a shower head right over the squat toilet in the bathroom. It had been installed a year ago in anticipation of Shan and his bride's visit. Lisha, "Lisa in English," was her name.

In the dining area of the room were a small dining table and a few chairs. These, still freshly painted red, and the headboard of the bed, the writing desk, the five-drawer dresser, the side-by-side closet in the bedroom, were among the pieces of furniture Mama Yao had prepared for Shan while he was still a junior at the university. The spring box and mattress were brand new, though. She had bought them for Shan and his bride. They had stayed for only a few days; three and a half days exactly.

Maliya nodded, bounced, cooed happily while touring the apartment. Her left hand fingers were intermingled with Dawei's right hand's, tapping lightly, as if playing an instrument; her head tilted slightly toward his shoulder, brushing it now and then. A big, adoring "YOU DID IT" look sparkled in her eyes whenever she turned to look at him.

"Everything's fantastic!" Maliya declared, both to Dawei and to Mama Yao.

"Well, this is your home now," Mama Yao said, before leaving, her eyes beaming with a joy she hadn't felt for a long while.

Yes, this was more like home now.

They—she and Principal Yao—had built this single-story brick farmhouse in the late 1970s. It was their second house. The first one, a small three-room thatched cottage, mud walls, mud floor, was built in the early 1960s, not long after their marriage. Its walls were disfigured by condemning posters during the Cultural Revolution, huge sheets of ghastly white paper, huge characters in wicked black ink, Principal Yao's name crossed out in dripping, blood-red paint. Three years after Principal Yao was "liberated," they decided to build a new home.

"You stay home," Mama Yao said breathlessly, when she saw her husband coming out with a spade. She was climbing up the slope of the new foundation with two big basketfuls of mud bouncing from a carrying pole on her right shoulder. With a raised foundation, brick walls, glass windows, and a thin layer of cement for the floor, there would be no more gaping rat holes in the ground, no more pale, skinny saplings growing under the bed or behind the closet.

"You stay home," she told him, when she was leaving for the commune's building material plant to pick bricks and shingles on fiercely hot, dusty summer evenings, not to pick the best ones—they could not afford them—but those over- or under-baked, to get discount prices.

His health had been ruined as a result of having been forced to kneel on broken glass for hours, then from being locked up in a dark, damp room for months.

They had planned four rooms. Two for themselves, two for Shan when he grew up and got married. Unfortunately, Principal Yao died less than a year after the new house was built. Since Shan went to college, he had rarely lived in the house, and since he went to America in the spring of '91, he hadn't come back to visit until just a year ago.

As Mama Yao was steaming pork and chive dumplings she had prepared early that morning, she heard talking and giggling from the other side of the wall. There was more life now. Not chilling silence day and night—oh, sure, there'd been echoes of her own steps, voices and music from the 19" Panda color TV, and wind whistling in the pitch darkness outside. Going to the neighbors' to play *majiang* helped a bit, yet at the end of the day, she still had to come home and face a big, empty house.

What would Dawei and Maliya have for supper? Would they know how to cook? She gathered a plateful of steamy dumplings and went knocking on their door.

"C'mon in, Mama Yao," Maliya said warmly after opening the door. On the dining table were two or three small paper boxes, already opened, a small cake with two lit candles, a bottle of champagne, a few white styrofoam cups. . . . They were in the middle of a celebration.

"Yes, join us, Mama Yao," Dawei echoed, standing up from his chair to greet her. "Mmm. . . I smell dumplings." He drew a long, deep breath into his nose: "Delicious!"

As soon as Mama Yao placed the steamy plate on the table, he picked up a dumpling, and threw it into his mouth.

"Wow, more delicious than my mom's," he declared, chewing noisily.

Maliya poured a cupful of champagne and handed it, with both hands, to Mama Yao.

"No. . . I don't drink," Mama Yao smiled.

"Just one cup, please," Maliya begged, giggling.

"And a slice of the cake, too!" Dawei joined.

"Okay, just one sip," Mama Yao gave in. It tasted cool, fruity, a bit pungent. The cake was so sweet, though. She felt a warmth welling up inside her.

"I've got more dumplings on the stove. Why don't you two continue?"

She went back, still feeling the champagne in her head. After finishing cooking, she sat down on the couch facing the TV and ate a few more dumplings, the most delicious she had had since. . . when?

The program she was watching was Holding Hands, a drama series she'd been following. She sighed when the thirtyish teacher-turned computer programmer decided to camp out in his tiny office littered with odd-shaped parts and cables. He'd just had a fallout with his wife who suspected him of having an affair with a young, beautiful associate.

When that night's episode was over, she watched a bit of

other programs, then dozed off on the couch, the prelude to going to bed almost every night.

About an hour later, as she got up and walked to the bedroom, sleepy-eyed, she heard the noise from the other side of the wall. She knew what that noise was. Only that you were supposed to keep your mouth shut, even if it meant biting your own lip; you were only supposed to hear that noise inside your head.

She had never even seen her fiancé—a young man three years older, from a neighboring village—until the wedding night. Well, that was not accurate. She had seen him once. From a distance. One day, while pulling weeds in the middle of a long rice field, her cousin called to her from a neighboring rice field:

"Look! There goes your young man!"

She raised her head, and saw the youthful back of her fiancé hurrying along the narrow mud road heading into town. She blushed all the way to her toes. She had heard that the young man was handsome—his skin was paler than that of city folks', and quite a scholar, too, one of the most gifted at the county's only middle school then.

Young people, nowadays. She yawned, pulling the blanket over her chest. Dawei and Maliya looked like a sweet pigeon pair, though. Besides, she had seen more blushing scenes on TV while visiting Shan in America. He was still a student then, living in a one-bedroom apartment in a graduate student compound. Since she couldn't go anywhere by herself, she spent a lot of time in front of the TV. Even though she didn't speak their language, she understood what she was watching. Mostly.

They came once or twice during the weekdays and stayed

for the weekends. Sometimes Dawei or Maliya would come over to use her phone. In the first few years while Shan was still a student in America, Mama Yao had to go to her husband's middle school to wait for her son's phone call. When it became possible for average folks to have phone services, Shan told his mother to go for it.

"It'd cost three thousand *yuan* just to install it. That's more than I can make in a whole year!"

"Money doesn't matter, Ma," Shan insisted.

Now he could call any time he wanted to. No more waiting for Mama Yao, either. One time, she had waited for almost a whole day in Principal Yao's former office. For a while, Shan called almost everyday. She made him call less—once every other day, every few days, then eventually, about once a week.

"Why not come and stay here everyday?" Mama Yao asked one day, when Maliya came to make a phone call.

"Don't want to get into trouble with the school," she said, mysteriously. "We're supposed to live in the dorms, you know. However, we're adults now, we should be able to live where we want to, right?"

Weekend mornings, the young couple had the habit of getting up late. Close to noon, Dawei would start to practice the violin. Shan used to do the same in that room, too. She didn't know how he had taken a fancy to that instrument or when he had gone into town to buy one. He didn't have a teacher or know anyone who knew how to play the violin, either. He just followed the two books he had bought and started to teach himself.

The first few days, it sounded real bad, like the squawking of a chicken being chased by a naughty cat. Weeks later, it sounded like someone just starting to learn to sing, hitting wrong notes all the time. Months later, the whole house would be singing melodies from the Eight Model Beijing Operas she had heard so often on the radio. Even the Twin-Sun River would seem to be murmuring along quietly, too. Passers-by would stop, as if enchanted, and ask Mama Yao, who was watering green vegetables in the garden.

"Yes, it's Shan," she would reply, beaming with pride.

Maliya would be practicing her English, too, standing like a statue under a persimmon tree thick with light orange fruit in the midst of deep green leaves, or pacing back and forth along the little brick path, her hands holding a book behind her back, murmuring in a birdlike, singing voice. Shan used to. . . .

"Stop it," Mama Yao told herself, "it's no use thinking like that all the time."

"Mama Yao," Maliya stopped pacing one day and asked when she saw her leaving for a few rounds of *majiang*. "Your son is teaching in a college in America?"

"Yes," Mama Yao replied, beaming.

"That's where I want to go, too." Maliya's eyes sparkled. "I want to go to a business school or law school there. You think I'll be able to?"

"Of course you can!" Mama Yao encouraged her.

Maliya resumed pacing along the brick path. Her murmuring seemed more determined, more eloquent now.

"Anytime you feel like cooking," Mama Yao would tell them, "help yourselves to any vegetables in my garden. They're so fresh! I don't use any chemical fertilizers, you know." Now and then, she'd leave a head of cabbage or a bunch of dewy, tender spinach, chives, or green onions at their door.

One evening a few days before the Mid-autumn Festival, Dawei and Maliya came over with a nice box of double-yolk moon cakes and wished her a happy holiday. When Maliya saw Mama Yao's swollen left cheek, she was concerned.

"It's the nagging toothache again," Mama Yao mumbled, with difficulty.

"My mother's a doctor," Maliya said. "I still have some pain killers left in my medicine box."

Maliya returned with a small bottle.

"'Ad-Vil joint venture product.'" She said. "Take one or two tonight before going to bed, one or two after breakfast tomorrow, the same tomorrow night, and you'll feel much better."

On the morning of the festival, Shan called. Lisha was on the phone, too. But she didn't speak Chinese, so Shan translated.

"Ma, I'm pregnant."

"What?"

"Lisha's pregnant. She's due in May."

"So I'll be Granny Yao soon?"

"Yes," Shan and Lisha confirmed, in chorus.

She walked with a light step all day that day. She had been waiting for the news for way too long.

"Ma, would you come and help take care of your grandchild?" Shan had asked. "We've just bought a new house and will be moving in this weekend. It won't be like the last time you visited."

"Sure," she answered, happily. Somewhere in the back of her mind, though, she wasn't sure: would she get along with Lisha?

That evening, Maliya came over.

"Did you see Dawei today, Mama Yao?"

"No, what happened? He's not home?"

"No. He said he would take care of something before coming back. We were supposed to be spending the holiday together, but it's already nine and he's still. . ."

"Oh, don't you worry. He may be tied up somewhere."

The next day, around noon, Mama Yao heard violin playing from the other side of the wall, like a spring swallow flying back to its nest, chanting rapturously. Through the kitchen window, she saw Maliya, in her knee-length red jacket, unbuttoned, pacing back and forth on the brick path, holding a book behind her back.

Just as the saying went, young couples fight at one end of the bed and patch it up at the other. Mama Yao smiled.

The same episode repeated itself a couple of times, with some variations here and there, but always ended the same.

In late October, when the persimmons looked almost golden, Mama Yao picked a small basketful for the young couple.

"They might still taste puckery. Let them sit there for a week or two and they'll be great," she reassured them.

Close to the end of the year, Mama Yao got word at a *majiang* table that the mayor was going to issue an order to ban renting rooms to college students.

"Why?" she asked.

"Because some people think it's morally wrong."

Her *majiang* friends urged her to talk to the mayor.

"Big sis," one of her friends, also widowed, said, "I know you are not renting for money, but you know I've got nobody else to depend on."

"Yes, go to talk to him, sis. Only you can change his mind," the other friends at the table pleaded.

Before supper that day, Mama Yao went to the mayor's residence, several houses down the cinder country road. It was a small walled compound, with a goose-egg shaped entrance guarded by a deep blue security door. She pressed the bell and after a few buzzes, the mayor's teenage daughter came and opened the door.

A wide footpath, paved with fine, colorful pebbles through the lush, well-manicured garden led her to the two-story building in the rear of the compound: red roof, beige stuccoed walls, spacious windows.

Shan would have been able to build such a residence if he had not gone to college, gone on to America. What would it be like to be living together with Shan, his wife, and her grandchild? Last year, during his visit, Shan had said he wanted to have a brand new house built for his mom. She shook her head.

"Why don't you come and live with us, then?"

Those humongous supermarkets, hot water available 24 hours a day, mild temperature inside the house (it didn't matter if the snow was mountain-high outside), and the clean, pure air you could breathe so freely. All that was great.

"But what could an old woman like me be doing there? Nobody to talk to, nobody to play *majiang* with, and no place I could go on my own?"

After having Mama Yao sit down in a shiny, squeaky leather sofa in the living room—twice bigger than her own—Mayor Lin handed her a Red Double-Happiness cigarette.

"You know I've quit for two years now. Shan insisted."

"Oh, now I remember. How is Shan?" The mayor had a slur in his speech, his mouth always seemingly on the verge of slobbering. This and the long, unsightly scar on the palm of his right hand were the result of being struck by a downed power line on a drizzly day when he, Shan, and a few other kids were playing outside. Shan had run for help, crying like the sky had fallen.

"He's fine. You know how he is." Mama Yao picked up the cup of Dragon Well tea the mayor had poured for her. After blowing away the few leaves still floating on the surface, gently, she sipped.

"I heard you wanted to ban having college kids as tenants. Is that true?" she asked, as if the question had just occurred to her.

A pause.

"Mama Yao, you know I'm caught in a real bad fix now," the mayor said, with obvious deference to the person who had sponsored his Party membership about fifteen years ago. He was still a young man then, with an uncertain future.

"Our village is now known as the Cohab Town, the butt of jokes for everybody," he sighed, shaking his head, before taking another drag from the cigarette. "Truth be told, nowadays I don't have the face to see anyone outside our village. I would try and find any excuse to avoid going to meetings in the county."

With a population of some 400 families, Twin-Sun River Village was just a couple of kilometers away from the teachers' college. Two years ago, when some college kids came to look for rooms to rent, nobody took them seriously. At first, one young man would rent a room and bring a girl to stay overnight now and then. Nobody really paid attention. But soon, it spread like wildfire.

Now, more than half of the families, creative enough to squeeze out some "surplus" space in their homes and turn it into some kind of efficiency, were making rental income steadily. A few eyebrows were raised, but in general, people just shrugged. With farmland being gobbled up like jellied bean curd by joint ventures and other new businesses, the villagers had been hard put to make a decent living. The extra rental income came in handy. Some of the more enterprising families had even opened up small eateries, groceries, and other businesses.

Everything had seemed fine. Until someone had stirred things up.

"I understand," Mama Yao said, sympathetically. "However, wouldn't it be more prudent to discuss it over with the masses before issuing any order?" She paused, then added, "After all, you're up for re-election next winter."

Mama Yao herself had been elected a county-level model worker and a delegate to its people's congress many times in her day.

"Tell me about it, Mama Yao," the mayor breathed heavily. "I'm under lots of pressure. The college president called me again yesterday. He told me that the students are required to stay in their dorms."

"The pains and itches of the masses are not to be overlooked, either. Right?" Mama Yao insisted.

The mayor nodded, blankly.

On a cold, windy evening two days later, a town hall meeting was held. The sole issue on the agenda was whether the college kids' tenancy should be continued. The turnout was unprecedented, even bigger than the hotly-contested mayoral election a year ago.

"These kids are what's wrong with our country today," an elderly man was the first to speak, punctuating his words emphatically with his smoky pipe. "People sleeping around, swapping spouses, marrying today and divorcing tomorrow. This country is going down the drain!"

"Yeah, the way they're running this country," another silver-haired man shouted in support, "the Long March might as well have never happened!"

"We don't want to forget, though," a fiftyish man donning a pair of thick glasses stood up to speak. Mama Yao recognized him as one of the middle school's history teachers. "These are not kids anymore. They are adults. As adults, they have the full constitutional right to live anywhere they want to and anyway they want to," he paused, "as long as they don't break any laws."

"But," a middle-aged woman in a thick, cotton-padded coat retorted, sheepishly, "the college has regulations, doesn't it? Aren't the students required to live in the—"

"We mind our business, the college minds its own," a ruddy-faced elderly woman, the first fiery revolutionary in the village to put up a big-character poster condemning the village leaders more than three decades ago, cut the middle-aged woman short, "and we'll leave the rest to the laws. If you can live by drinking northwestern wind and morality, sis, go ahead. I can't."

"Who can? Who?" a few villagers shouted, craning their heads to look around the town hall.

Silence.

"What if they make babies?" an old woman, her face all

wrinkled up, her head having only a few listless white hairs left, mumbled in a corner.

"That means their parents have got themselves an early promotion," the village's accountant, a man known for his quick wit, teased, "and you, granny, get to baby-sit again."

The town hall broke into a light-hearted laugh.

"Well, seriously," a young man in the front row raised his hand, uncertainly, "I've heard of all these horrible diseases. I mean, what if they spread to us?"

"Young man," snapped the accountant, good-humoredly, "If you keep your pants on all the time, I'll guarantee you'll be safe."

The town hall roared with laughter again.

Finally, the issue was put to a vote. After the votes were counted: 46 voted to keep things as they were, 38 voted to ban student tenants. There were 16 abstentions.

Mayor Lin wiped away the sweat oozing on his forehead with a huge, white handkerchief.

Mama Yao sighed with relief, too.

When she got back home after the meeting, it was very late. She was still feeling the excitement. Life had certainly become more complicated than it used to be. Yeah, what if they made babies? What if someone caught those diseases? Weren't students supposed to follow their school's regulations? She didn't have clear answers. Well, these questions are too heavy for an old woman to think about at this late hour, she told herself.

She turned on the TV and sat on the couch. *Holding Hands* had ended about a month ago. She was following a new drama series, but its broadcast time was from eight to nine in the evening.

She decided to watch a late night show called *For Whom Does Your Heart Beat?* In this show, groups of young men and women were playing a game to match their personalities and hobbies. The most compatible pairs would go out on a date.

After a while, the game got a bit confusing and her eyelids felt heavy. She knew she would be dozing off soon. As she was falling into the hazy twilight between consciousness and sleep, she picked up a conversation—a sort of shouting match, though the voices were muffled.

"Why did you go out with her last night?" a fluty girl's voice questioned.

"To see a movie, *The Titanic*," a low-pitched young man's voice replied. "You saw it already, long time ago."

"Why did you? It was Christmas Eve, for God's sake!"

"How could I refuse. . . ."

Silence.

"Because she's cuter, her eyes are bigger, shinier?"

"C'mon, don't make a big deal. . . ."

"What about Rachel?"

"What about her?"

"Think I didn't know? Where did you spend your Mid-autumn Festival night?"

"With you, of course!"

"You didn't come back until after midnight!"

"So?"

"Just because the way she swings her hips at dance parties?"

"At least she won't whine!"

"I could smell that bitch on your clothes, your body, from a kilometer away that night. I almost threw up!"

This is getting bad, Mama Yao thought, drowsily.

"Think I don't know what *you*'ve been up to, too?" It was the young man's turn to question.

"What?"

"Wednesday evening, in a corner on the second floor of the library—"

"What?"

"—you and Tom, your heads almost touching. What a nice picture! Thought nobody'd see you!"

"So, you've been following me?"

"Just as you've been checking on me!"

"You. . . .I was just helping him review grammar. . .present perfect, past perfect. . . ."

"Like I'd believe you."

Sniffling.

A long sigh escaped her lips as Mama Yao stirred on the couch.

"You don't love me any more."

"I. . . . who's ever talked about love? You know several girls had asked me, but I picked you. . . *you*!"

"Your conscience has been eaten by dogs!"

"Conscience? You mean I'm supposed to be grateful? Just because your dad and mom have more money and you pay more than half of the rent?"

"You. . . you son of a. . . ."

Things were thrown around, crashing.

Sobbing.

Mama Yao sat up in the couch, as if dazed, trying to shake off the haze in her head.

"Remember the understanding? No obligation?"

"To hell with the understanding!"

"Okay, from now on, you follow your broad, sunlit road to America, I'll stick to my single-board bridge to starvation, as a poor music teacher!"

A few more things thrown, crashing.

What a mess, Mama Yao thought to herself, opening her eyes.

Longitudinal stripes of red, blue, orange, green, yellow, were raining down the screen in the midst of harsh static hissing from the set.

Eerie silence on the other side of the wall.

Would the couple be able to patch it up at the other end of the bed this time?

All seemed quiet the following morning. Mama Yao had an early lunch, and went out. At the end of yesterday's town hall meeting, her *majiang* friends had asked her to go over and play a few rounds today. She didn't come back until late in the afternoon.

It had snowed. Two or three centimeters, perhaps. It was enough to dress up the whole world in a thin layer of pure, shiny white. It hadn't snowed much these years. Not since Shan was small. Those knee-deep snow days seemed to be gone. What did they say, El Nino? What was that?

As she trudged along the country road, her cheeks could feel whiffs of cold air from the Twin-Sun River.

Something was not quite right. What was it? She couldn't name it.

When she got to the entrance of her bushy fence, she knew exactly why.

The tracks left by a car she had seen on the way home ended

right there. Messy, mixed with lots of footprints.

She hurried home, knocked on the apartment's door. Nobody answered. She fumbled in her purse, found the spare key, which she had never used since the kids had moved in, and opened the door.

"Anybody home?" she shouted.

No answer.

Nobody in the kitchen.

Nobody in the bathroom.

On the small fresh red dining table were a key, two 100-*yuan* bills, and a slip of white paper with the word "Thanks!" on it, apparently written in a big hurry.

She went inside the bedroom. The sea blue bag, the rosy red suitcase. . . were all gone. On the floor, though, were a few sheets of paper, torn, stamped on. By the few rays of sunshine slanted through the window, she could make out those long, flowery bean sprouts and strange-looking English words on their wrinkled surfaces.

As she bent to pick them up, she caught sight of something else under the edge of the bed, something flimsy, fragile, golden, abandoned on the cold cement floor.

She knew what it was. It was broken. The heart-shaped ruby stone was nowhere in its vicinity.

She stared at it for a long while.

When she came out to lock up the apartment, her eyes blinked in the glittering, almost dazzling rays of the setting sun sieved through the snow-covered bare brunches of the persimmon trees.

It occurred to her that Shan hadn't called for over a week.

Old Batteries

Ten thousand thanks, your honor, for allowing me to speak for myself today. I don't know where my attorney is. Either he's wetted his bed again, couldn't find his pants, or his alarm clock isn't working. Since he isn't here, I figured someone had to say something. Under the circumstances, that solemn responsibility has to be mine and mine solely.

Wow, your honor, I'm a bit nervous; a long-time junkie of crime stories, TV drama, movies, what have you . . . first time defendant in court myself, in the celestial presence of someone like you. What? Don't be modest. I'm mighty proud of modesty, one of the glorious Chinese virtues, but sometimes we flaunt that virtue just a tiny bit too . . . wouldn't you agree?

Well, your honor, please allow me to cut to the chase, without wasting your precious time on any unnecessary preambles. First and foremost, I confess that I've committed a horrible crime, and I . . . I deserve to die by a thousand cuts. That's really how I feel, I swear by my humble honor the absolute truth of this statement. I'll swear to the Old Man . . . No? No swearing in court? I'm terribly sorry. I'm still a bit nervous. Let me take a long, deep breath, easy, easy, there, that's better.

Please, your honor, allow me to begin again. I was saying that I've committed a horrible crime, but somehow I don't know what hit me that day. Really, it was like I'd blacked out. Even if you strike me with Five Thunders, crush me to tiny pieces with Heaven, I wouldn't be able to recall a thing. I'm willing to swear the absolute truth to the Old . . . huh? No swearing in court. I meant to say, it doesn't matter how hard I try to track it down, whenever I get just a tiny bit closer, the memory of that day would be shying off, furtive, like a guilt-struck ghost.

Umm, speaking of ghosts, that reminds me of something, an experience I had when I was a kid, about twelve years old, give or take. That was so long ago, during my previous incarnation. What? No ghosts in court, your honor? I promise there's a connection with . . . I can continue? Ten thousand thanks, your honor! You are the wisest, the most brilliant . . . no flattery in court, either? I'm sorry, but that was from the bottom of my heart.

Well, to make a long story short, this is what happened: One day, at the end of the afternoon class, my language teacher came to my desk and gave me a ticket for the *Little Flower Girl*, to be shown that evening. Remember that North Korean movie? You know what this meant, during those days when there wasn't much real entertainment, except for, of course, those Eight Model Beijing Operas. You look like my age, your honor, so I won't bore you with what you already know.

She said only one pupil from each class could go. I was thrilled. I mean, she, my teacher, was the prettiest thing I'd ever set my eyes on. City girl, creamy skin as soft as . . . freshly-made bean curd, eyes that could speak directly to your heart. She liked to pace around the classroom, aisle by aisle, from front to back, when she led us in reading from the *Little Red Book* in chorus. She'd hold the book in front of her, pacing around; her movement was so gentle, her voice was so bird-like, I mean, whenever she got close to me, whenever her clothes brushed the edge of my desk, slightly, like the wings of a butterfly, I'd smell a faint whiff of her; not any perfume or colored chemical stuff girls like to spray on themselves nowadays, but the faint whiff of her true, natural self. Oh my, a little rabbit would be bouncing in my young heart, my face would be blushing like it was on fire.

I confess, your honor, I did have a big crush on her. Can I trust you, though, your honor, that this tiny morsel from my past life would not be chewed at dinner tables beyond the walls of this court? And it wouldn't affect the outcome of this trial, one way or the other? After all, a citizen's privacy and dignity is at stake here. Right?

Well, as I said, I won't bore you with the details of the movie, either. I did cry my heart out, dabbing my eyes with my little dirty handkerchief after using it to blow my nose I don't know how many times. After all, my pretty teacher and just about everybody else around me were crying themselves into mud puddles. And right in front of my eyes was this lovely, innocent little proletarian sister who suffered horribly in the hands of those stonehearted reactionaries and capitalists. I mean, for God's sake, that damned pot of hot, boiling water being poured over her eyes? Those dogs-won't-eat bastards! Sorry, that was just a slip of the tongue.

Your honor, please allow me to get to the heart of the story, without any further preambles. When the movie was over, it was close to midnight. After saying goodbye to my pretty teacher and other lucky schoolmates, I was on my way home. That means I had to walk for miles on a narrow, windy dirt country road along the Tri-Forked River. It was pitch dark. I mean, there was nothing illuminating the world between heaven and earth in the country on that night. I couldn't even see my own five fingers at arm's length.

For the first ten minutes or so, it wasn't too bad. That little flower girl, the pretty teacher, and my schoolmates were still with me. You know what I mean? By and by, though, I became worried. I knew I was getting closer to the place.

It was a two or three-hundred-meter strip between the road and the river, covered by twisty branches of dead willows, marshes of tall, wild reeds, and monstrous weeds that looked as if they were injected by some weird growth hormones.

In the midst of this, half-hidden, and half-peeping, were those little mounds of mud graves, grandpa-sized, baby-sized, freshly made ones, and really old ones, so old that I had fancied, on my way to the movie theater earlier that day, catching glimpses of white bones in some broken, rotting coffins.

It had made my flesh creep hours earlier when the late afternoon sun was still hanging over the tip of the Tiger Mountain in the west. Imagine now at this ghostly hour, me, a moustache-less kid, passing this ghostly place alone, not even accompanied by my own shadow, or a single ray of moonlight. Oh, occasionally, I did see a glowworm or two blinking in the marshes or somewhere. I was too scared to whistle even though I was already damned good at it. I just held my breath and tiptoed ahead, like in a real bad dream. Boy, that must have been harder than the Long March, with all due respect.

You know what was on my mind, what I was wishing for, when I was treading past that ghostly place? A flashlight! Yes, a flashlight. That'd have made all the difference. Wouldn't you agree?

I didn't pray, I didn't know how anyway, but that wish of mine was granted a year later.

My maternal uncle, a chief mechanic at an electronic plant in the provincial capital, came to visit. Usually, he'd just bring me a few candies. That had been quite a treat already. That day, however, he brought me a flashlight. A flashlight! A used one, but it didn't matter because it was still working.

Imagine how I'd fuss with it, unscrewing its head, removing the round glass cover, taking out the little bulb and the two D-sized batteries, putting them all back. At night, I'd push the tip of my nose real hard, upward with my left thumb, grin hard, showing as much teeth as I could, while shining the flashlight on my face from below the chin. Oh, how the ghostly face in my mother's mirror would scare me!

I'd also stick the flashlight's head against either side of my left palm and shine it. My fingers would look so pinkish-red, so translucent, I'd see blood pulsating in the veins.

My most favorite game, though, was to flash the light into the vast, endless sky. It'd go up and up for a few hundred meters, then disappear into the darkness. What'd it be like to climb up that pole of light? Would it get me to the moon, to the stars?

I was so fascinated by that thought. It made me worried, too. What if somebody down on earth played a trick on me by turning off the flashlight while I was still up there, climbing? What if the battery ran out? Are you still with me, your honor? You're so kind.

That worry about crashing to a premature death alarmed me to something else: if I played with the flashlight just a bit too much, the batteries would be gone soon. So, I put it in an old shoebox and hid it under the bed. Every time I felt the urge to take it out, my fingers got real itchy, I'd tell myself to go get lost. I'd drag myself outside and try and find other interesting things to occupy myself. Gradually, my mind did wander off to other things, like making my own slingers, playing glass balls, searching for sparrow nests under the eaves of folks' thatched roofs.

Then, about a year later, when my mom said uncle was coming to visit us again, that reminded me of something. I crawled under the bed and got out the shoebox.

The flashlight somehow felt different. I couldn't name it. A bit heavier, perhaps. I pressed the button, no light came out. It didn't matter how many times and how hard I pressed. I tried to unscrew the head; it was stuck. I figured it was due to the rust that could be seen around the metal tube's edges. So I found the old family lamp. A few drops of kerosene later it loosened up like magic.

Then, the batteries wouldn't come out. I grabbed their edges with my fingers and pulled real hard. They wouldn't give. I shook, I cussed, I begged. It didn't work either. They must have fed themselves some weird growth hormones or something, I mean, they'd gobbled up all the space between themselves and the tube. Eventually, using a vise, I did succeed in dragging them out.

They looked terrible, I mean they had white, sticky powder all over them. I figured the dampness under the bed was the real culprit. You remember the kind of houses we used to live in back then, mud walls, mud floor. . . .

To make a long story short, that was why and how a year ago I started to collect dead batteries.

I'm not going to bore you with the stories of how I made

money, how I turned reeds and willow twigs into cute baskets and sold them in a store in the county, how I hit a gold pot one summer day when two foreigners, a man and a woman, wandered into my store. The man was tall and muscular; his hands, his legs, his face were so hairy, I mean, as hairy as a bear or . . . a monkey or something. His wife was so pretty, I mean her eyes were so blue, like one of those glass balls I used to play with. Both smelt a bit; perhaps they had drunken too much sheep's milk. But they were such nice people. They looked at all the baskets on display, talked to me—well, their mouths moved, they made wild gestures, they wrote figures on a sheet of paper. I didn't understand a thing they said. Yet strangely, I understood. That's how I started my export business.

The long and short of it is that I didn't go to college, I tried the college entrance exam once in '77 and failed miserably, not the kind of material, you know. But I had become rich, rich enough to build a brand new home—a two-story residence, brick walls, cement floors, hardwood stairs to the second floor, air conditioning. Your honor, I didn't mean to brag in your celestial presence because your residence must be a thousand times fancier. No? How come? Okay, okay, I'll get back to my story.

In the county, I rented a much bigger, spacious place for my basket export business, completely renovated, wallpaper décor, ceramic floor, display room downstairs, office upstairs, with a phone, a fax, and even a computer, huge windows overlooking the busy streets. I even bought myself a car and a truck. I mean, I was doing okay. I'd gained weight, and my beer belly would cast a shadow on the floors of karaoke halls almost every night. I felt life was good.

But somehow I became bored, you know what I mean? Like

there wasn't much in life that'd interest me any more. Even the most expensive delicacies in the world would not give me any appetite. Not like when I was a kid. You were always hoping for something, a new jacket for the New Year, a new flashlight, you know what I mean.

Then one day, as I stretched out in the leather sofa in my office, thumbing through the pages of the day's newspaper, my daily routine, you know, a cup of the freshest Dragon Well tea on the glass coffee table, something in a headline caught my eye. It seemed to strike some sort of chord in me.

I read the story. It was about how people just dumped dead batteries all over the place, how the mercury in them could really hurt the environment, that sort of stuff. I flew into a rage. How'd people just do things like that? So stupid, so uncivilized, so. . . you know.

As I sighed and turned in the sofa and sipped tea, it came to me, like being lost on a long, pitch-dark country road and suddenly seeing light not too far ahead: here's something a proud citizen of the People's Republic like me could do to make a difference. You remember the saying? The rise and fall of the nation is in the hands of every doggie, sorry, every common citizen? Something like that? I mean, I'd just stumbled upon a new purpose in life.

The next morning, I put out a big sign in the display window of my business:

Old Batteries Recycled Here

Nobody responded. I mean, for days, nobody brought in a single battery. Then, it dawned on me that this is market economy now and you've got to give people incentives to do anything. So, I made up a new sign:

Old Batteries Recycled: Five Cents Apiece

Wow, have I touched a magic button or something. A few kids came right after the new sign was up, got paid twenty cents here and a *yuan* or two there.

Then, more kids, then adults, even old grannies, swarmed down like bees. Man, everybody and his brother now wanted to help with the environment.

Speaking of the environment, I remember going to Nanning to see its famed mountains and waters. You must know that saying, Nanning mountains and waters are the most beautiful between heaven and earth? Even the Clintons. . . No? That's Guilin? Sorry, I shouldn't have shown off my little learning in your most erudite presence.

At any rate, I was saying, at the end of a long day of following little paths to mist-capped ridges and sailing in crystal blue waters, I went downtown to look for a place to satisfy my hunger. Really, you don't need to look far. Restaurants, eateries, food stands were just about everywhere. I was dazzled and couldn't make up my mind.

Then, I caught sight of a young girl, sixteen or seventeenish, outside a fancy- looking restaurant. She had a real nice figure, slender, supple, wrapped in a real nice red silk *qipao*; its slit skirt and the long golden sash across her shoulders were fluttering in the evening breeze. The sight of her standing there, greeting prospective customers, with the cutest smile I'd ever set eyes on. It made your heart feel so. . . so itchy; it made you ache so deliciously for her. I mean even you, your honor, wouldn't have had the strength to resist. So, I became one of her willing captives.

Once inside, a thick, rich aroma, somehow different from anything I had known before, greeted my nose. There were twenty some tables. Most of them were already occupied. The hostess, another young and pretty girl, took me to a table in a corner and then asked me what I'd like.

"What do you recommend?" I asked.

They were serving a special, something called the Manchu-Han Complete Banquet.

"What is it?" I asked, curiously.

"Well," she began, "it's something the emperors of the Qing Dynasty used to like. Nowadays, even average folks like you can enjoy. . .on a much smaller scale, of course." She winked her right eye and cocked her head just a tiny bit at the table right next to mine.

The table—two men and two women were sitting around it—had six or seven steamy dishes, a few of those cute little wine cups with "Ten Thousand Years and More" printed on them, and some odd-looking, real sharp metal utensils. The oddest thing was that right in the middle, in a big stainless steel plate, was a small, long-tailed monkey, the size of a little puppy; it was squatting there, in a dreamy, drowsy, half-drunk kind of state.

Was the monkey a sort of ornament? I asked.

"No," the girl explained, "it's actually the highlight of the banquet."

"Huh!?"

"Well, you'll find out," the girl cooed. "Monkey brains, eaten with pickled ginger, chili sauce, and good wine. You'd feel like you're in heaven."

I couldn't believe my ears. I mean, I'd been to places, and eaten all sorts of things, pigeons, frogs, dogs, turtles, even snakes, but had never heard of this one.

"The fun part of it is," the girl continued, "you get to choose your own monkey, too."

I wasn't sure that was what I'd do. But curiosity got the better of me. What's that saying? Once you're here, you might as well relax and enjoy the best you can? So, I followed the girl to the back of the restaurant, she lifted a heavy greasy curtain for me, and there we were, inside a storage room.

It was not bigger than my garage and was lit by a greenish florescent light. It had a real strong, offensive, urine-like smell. Cramped along the walls and on the floor were tanks and tanks of live fish, turtles, snakes, and what have you. And yes, there were quite a few cages of long-tailed monkeys, too.

This place made my skin feel real creepy. I mean, me, who had eaten all kinds of stuff, had even seen an old water buffalo being slaughtered? Well, I'd have to save that story for another day.

As I was saying, I was led to a cage which contained five or six long-tailed monkeys. They were all lined up there, their humanlike faces were pressed hard against the bars of the cage.

Watching.

Waiting.

Suddenly, all hell broke loose. Shrill screaming, chasing, jumping, running, flying up and down. Real commotion. In less than ten seconds, the dust settled and the battle was over.

Three or four big, strong monkeys pushed a much smaller one to the cage door. It was gasping for air.

I looked into the loser's eyes: they were shiny, filled with terror. In that pair of eyes, distorted by terror, I saw myself. I was frightened. I turned and ran. I ran out of the storage room, and out of the restaurant. I ran as fast as my two trembling legs could carry me.

You know, your honor, I had once been held like that. I was a fifth grade kid, then. My father's father had been a landowner before '49. You know what that'd mean during the Cultural Revolution. What's that saying? As dragons give birth to dragons, pheasants give birth to pheasants, so do heroes father good men, and reactionaries father rascals? I apologize for parading these old relics in your honor's celestial presence, again. Couldn't help it, though.

One day the village and our school were going to have a denunciation rally against my father and all the other ghosts and bad cows. When I heard the announcement, I bolted for the door. Two or three big bullies gave chase, caught me before I reached the school's gate. They grabbed my arms, twisted them all the way back, up in the air, and marched me back to the classroom.

I couldn't see my eyes then, but I bet you the terror in them must have looked like those of the little monkey.

I mean, for God's sake, our Chinese civilization is the greatest in the world. You know that I know that everybody knows that. Yet some of our folks behave like barbarians. I mean, why the monkeys? Aren't they supposed to be our ancestors, some millions of years ago? Eating monkey brains—wouldn't that make us cannibals?

Yeah, I know, I read somewhere that some Americans like to eat deer testicles and other weird animal parts, too. But aren't we the most glorious civilization and supposed to be a gleaming beacon of hope for the rest of the world?

I apologize, your honor, for having been carried away in my fit of passion. I'll get to the point in a second. I know you are extremely busy and have other important cases to hear today.

As I was saying, our beloved motherland has changed, people are much more environmentally conscious now. Nowadays, when I take a cruise ship vacation down the Yangtze, I don't see much of the same old blue, brown, or golden industrial waste being pumped into the river any more. Thousands of those small plants have been shut down.

Still remember that paper plant outside the county? Even from miles away, you could smell it: sour, choking, making it difficult for you to breathe; it would leave a layer of cinder-like dust on the leaves of vegetables in the garden.

No wonder my father, who had survived the Cultural Revolution, died of lung cancer a few years later. He never had a chance to live in the new residence I've built. He wasn't a smoker, a drinker, or anything like that. Now my uncle is dying of the same killer illness. Too many good people I know, neighbors, teachers, childhood friends, have gone that way.

I know, I know, things are getting better, but much more drastic measures need to be taken; otherwise, we'd all be endangered species soon, wouldn't you agree, your honor?

Anyway, back to the batteries. They came in plastic bags, cardboard boxes, and willow baskets. All kinds, all sizes. Some even had fancy foreign words on them. They must have traveled a long way before ending up at my place. I had tested a few, out of sheer curiosity, and they could still give a weak, yellowish light.

In just a few weeks, the batteries had taken up all the space downstairs, crawled upstairs, and taken over my office.

I'm not complaining. I mean, I'd started it all myself. Nobody had pointed a gun at me and said:

"Collect those damned batteries or I'll blow your brains out!"

Besides, though I wasn't in this to become a celebrity, the story they carried in the local newspaper pleased me quite a bit. Right after that, a female reporter from the province capital daily came to interview me, too. They even sent down a TV crew. That was the first time I'd ever appeared on TV. Imagine, your honor, someone as common as me on TV? I wish my old man had been alive to see me grinning from ear to ear on the tube. That'd have meant something.

Before I knew it, though, every inch of breathing space in my office, from floor to ceiling, was gone. I decided to ship truckloads of dead batteries home, to store them, temporarily, in my beautiful two-story residence in the country. But they kept coming. I was like a monstrously big magnet and bags and bags of dead batteries from nowhere and from everywhere were being sucked in my direction. Some bags showed patches of sticky, brownish powder on the outside. They smelt real stinky, too.

I became alarmed. I went to the county's environmental affairs office; I went to recycling factories; I even went to the provincial capital, to beg for help.

Everybody I saw was real nice, full of praise for my noble, patriotic sacrifices, but nobody, I mean *nobody* offered to help. They just shrugged. Either they didn't have the technical knowhow to recycle dead batteries, the funds to develop such knowhow, or they didn't have the space to store them.

In the meantime, my old mother, my wife, and my son

were bugging me everyday. Why? Because my beautiful home had become a graveyard:

"When are you going to get rid of those damned batteries?"

"You won't be happy until you've killed us all?"

They wailed at me like that every day. My son's fiancée had given him an ultimatum, too:

"Me or the batteries!"

On the evening of the fifteenth, after hearing their grief for the hundredth time over the phone, I just lost myself, your honor. I had difficulty breathing. I kept hearing shrill condemnations in my head. I felt like being crushed to meat pies under mountains of dead batteries.

I've got to do something. I've got to do something. I kept telling myself, doubling up in the sofa.

I rolled off the sofa, climbed out of the office, tripped my way downstairs, and grabbed a bag here, a box there, whatever I could lay my hands on, and dragged them to my truck. When the pile on the truck couldn't go any higher, I jumped into the truck, floored the gas pedal, and roared away.

The two beams of light from the truck cut into the pitch-darkness ahead like long sharp swords, but I was blinded by an animal-like rage. I didn't have the faintest idea where I was going, yet I was going somewhere. No, I was just wandering around like a headless ghost.

That, your honor, is as much as I can recall.

Your honor, for the life of me, I'd never imagined that I'd do something so horrible. That'd be the last place I'd have chosen to dump those damned batteries. So quiet, so beautiful now, no more dead willows, no more reed marshes, no more monstrous weeds, just well-manicured green grass, perennials, and evergreen plants.

Yes, your honor, all the evidence against me is as undisputable as the Tiger Mountain outside the county. I've committed a horrible crime against the ghosts of our ancestors. It's a crime that deserves death by a thousand cuts.

However, your honor, given the testimonies I've just presented, I hereby solemnly plead not guilty of the charges against me, on the reason of temporary insanity.

I plead for a chance to make amends to the ancestral ghosts by cleaning up the cemetery by the Tri-Forked River so that they could rest in peace.

I plead for a chance to devote the rest of my life and . . . all of the money I've made to the noble cause of turning dead batteries into treasures.

Whatever you do, your honor, just don't send my ass to a cold and lonely jail cell. This body isn't too old yet, and this patriotic heart is still beating strong.

Please, your honor, give me a chance to prove to the Old Man that I'm just as worried for my motherland as he was, when he was still a youngster, standing on the tip of the Orange Island, watching the Yangtze River flowing eastward, pondering how to cure her ills:

A thousand hills being crimsoned,
Their deep woods richly dyed
A hundred barges racing
Over crystal blue waters,
Eagles. . .

What? Not the Yangtze River? I've exceeded my time? My attorney's finally arrived? That turtle's son, what's taken him so long to crawl here?

What? You've just returned from a trip to Nanning? You're having a bad cough and temperature? But my ass has been on the chopping board!

A thousand apologies, your honor, that just slipped out. Please completely disregard whatever nonsense I've just said in this last half hour.

Now, you sons of turtles. How shall we plead to the judge? I can't hear you. Why are you wearing a gauze mask, for God's sake? A weird epidemic is . . . What?

Love Me, Love My Dog

He hated dogs. He still had a string of peanut size odd-shaped scars on the right side of his butt to remind him of his hatred every now and then, particularly when he needed to strip naked to bathe or take a quick shower.

Naturally, Dalong Li was not very fond of women in expensive-looking fur coats, genuine or artificial, who, with noses tilted up toward the sky, paraded through the streets with a little puppy in their arms or on a long, false diamond-studded leash. Who did they think they were? Cindy Crawford, Vanessa Williams, or whoever the world's super-most super model might be, promenading down the Fifth Avenue in Manhattan or the Champs-Elysées in Paris?

Besides, there were millions of humans, like those skinny, bony, big-headed kids in Somalia and Sudan he had seen on TV, who had to suffer the pangs of hunger everyday.

These women could certainly use a good lecture to knock some human sense into their airy heads, he thought.

Although Dalong had never expressed his strong, dog-related sentiment in words, his wife, college-educated and overly sensitive to his well-nuanced body language, should have inferred as much from the look in his eyes or the little, dismissive grunt that escaped his nose whenever the couple saw a woman in the company of her puppy drifting toward them in the crowded streets.

That was why he was shocked beyond speech one mid-summer afternoon when he came back from a weeklong business trip. As usual, he parked the Santana 2000 in the driveway, grabbed his briefcase and luggage bag, hurried up the stone-steps, and pressed the doorbell.

"Freeze! Hands up!" His wife's pigeon-like voice commanded when the door half opened.

Yet instead of the sweet smile in a face he had become so accustomed to for the last fifteen years, Dalong saw something quite different:

The eyes were okay: dark, oval, and exuding the same intelligent alertness he had learned to appreciate from his wife.

The forehead, well, was moderately rounded, the cheeks smooth, the nose straight, and the chin cute and defined.

But why all this mountainous cloud of fluffy, puffy creamy-colored fur bouncing from the head down to the ears to the shoulders, for Heaven's sake? This was July and he could hear the central air unit humming laboriously in the background. Some kind of joke?

The face looked elegant all right, even a bit regal, but it was only remotely human, and it was suspiciously doggish.

"Meet Louis, honey!" A familiar, smiling face popped out from behind the enormously furry doggish head.

Louis! Louis Who? Louis XVI? Louis XVII? Which one had the luck to lose his head to a guillotine? But a lost head was a lost head was a lost head, and it didn't concern him as urgently as the head he was facing now.

Louis was being thrust into his face again. Startled by the

sudden proximity to a not so friendly human face, the dog barked.

His wife giggled mirthfully. Even though she was fast approaching her fortieth birthday, her giggle still had that girlish kind of ring which never failed to stir up something warm inside him, some sweet, distant memory.

He was cooking eggs with an electric cup in his messy, crowded dorm room shared with five other students when he heard an outburst from behind:

"Freeze! Hands up!"

He whirled around and almost knocked over the steamy cup when he faced the origin of that outburst, a pretty girl in a light yellow blouse and a long, creamy skirt. She was giggling so heartily, her right hand reaching out with her thumb and index finger wide open as if pointing a pistol at him.

Poor him! He was still in his shorts, sweaty, and stripped from waist up.

His blind date had arrived one full hour too early.

That was then. This sudden, unexpected dog situation he was facing now, however, was a whole new, different ball game. It was, in fact, quite a matter of principle, and when had he ever compromised on matters of principle?

A not so kind comment, in the form of a question, leapt on to the tip of his tongue, but Dalong swallowed it back instantly. If one and a half decades of matrimonial bliss and bitter fights had taught him anything, it would be to swallow an inopportune statement voluntarily before it had a chance to be made in the heat of the moment rather than be forced to take it back after it had found its intended ears.

He grinned, ambiguously, instead.

That was how he was introduced to Louis, the newest member of his family.

"Mama Han," his wife hollered to the kitchen. "Monsieur is back."

"Monsu?" Mama Han, their live-in domestic, a fiftyish woman, popped out her head from inside the kitchen. "Who's Monsu?"

"Dalong, his new name from today on!" There was still a hint of giggle in his wife's pigeon-like voice.

That meant his wife would be "Madame" too? he mused.

"Just about everyone I know, their dog is either Thomas, Margaret, or George," crooned Madame at the dinner table half an hour later. "So common, and boring. I want my pet to be really unique. One of a kind, you know. Besides, he's a poodle. The national dog of France!" She placed the ivory chopsticks back on the huge, glass top dining table, picked up Louis, held him feelingly in her arms, tight against her semi-translucent silky blouse, and dodged, giggling, as Louis tried to lick her face with his long, wet tongue.

He looked up from his bowl, was conscious of a tinge of warm jealousy rushing up into his cheeks, but washed it down with a sip of iced Heineken from a tall glass. No, he didn't want to appear petty. That would be unbecoming of him.

So the last semester in college of struggling with "*Comment vous appelez-vous?*" and "*Parlez-vous français?*" and le tableau de conjugations to fulfill the second foreign language requirement was not a complete waste after all.

But he, Monsieur, and his wife, Madame? A bit too

pretentious, too petty bourgeoisie, wasn't it? Would Monsieur and Madame have to kowtow to Louis— XVI? XVII?—from now on as his loyal subjects and servants?

These little misgivings, however, were not strong enough to spoil his overall good mood as he sat in the soft-cushioned arm chair in the spacious dining room enjoying the five-course plus soup dinner Mama Han had prepared, under Madame's direct supervision, of course.

He liked the feeling of driving home at the end of a long, tiring day, slowing down at the gate of the upscale residential compound, watching without appearing to be watching the uniformed security man saluting with eyes as the shiny, black compressible door slid open, the kind of respect he had seen paid exclusively to the motorcade of national leaders or foreign dignitaries just a few years back, and cruising along a curvy, tree-lined road dotted on both sides with two or three-story single homes and condominiums, all stones and bricks, grand, with garages, balconies, and lush, well-manicured lawns. It gave him a sense of accomplishment, the feeling that he had arrived. He had taken a risk, a calculated risk, in giving up the comfortable job as the assistant director of the Office of Economic Policy Studies of the municipal government and starting a business of his own, and had been rewarded richly.

He sipped from the cool, sweaty tall glass again.

"Dal. . . Monsu," Mama Han asked in her heavy Anhui accent. "How do you like the new salad dish? Mad . . . Madame says seaweed is good for you."

"Excellent!" He nodded vaguely, a smile on his face.

Mama Han had been with them for almost two years now. With this arrangement, his wife could have more time to relax and pursue her hobbies a bit more rigorously: shopping, playing *majiang* with her friends, and leisure reading. She had been complaining about a general, nondescript fatigue ever since their son was born.

Madame picked up a large piece of juicy, sweet and sour pork with her chopsticks and brought it to Louis' mouth. Louis grunted excitedly when his long, wet tongue was in contact with the rib. Madame released the dog, who immediately went under the dining table to grabble with the rib noisily.

Mama Han frowned imperceptibly despite the faint, forced smile on her face.

He—Monsieur—managed to remain noncommittal in his facial expression.

"Poodle comes in three sizes, you know," Madame crooned again, picking up an itsy-bitsy piece of well-cooked dove wing from the plate, chewing deliberately. "The standard. The miniature. The toy. With moderation being my philosophy, I went for the miniature."

Moderation being her philosophy! Louis must have cost close to ten thousand *yuan*, an average worker's income for a whole year, plus registration, another ten thousand *yuan*, perhaps. He had heard his business partners and associates bragging about how much they had spent acquiring such foreign dogs. Yet . . . yet what was the purpose of making money if it were not to make his family happy?

Later that night, when all had quieted down and even the cicadas in the trees outside had quit singing their carefree songs, he and his wife settled in their queen-sized bed in the master bedroom upstairs.

Just when he finally got into the act of reconnecting with his wife, conjugally, he heard a string of baby-like whining noises at the door.

"I thought you had put it, I mean Louis, inside the crate in the storage room?" He mumbled, sweatily.

"I," his wife murmured, apologetically. "I was afraid that Louis would feel too confined, claustrophobic, you know?"

He disengaged and turned to his side of the bed as his wife—Madame—slid out of bed to take care of poor Louis.

A few nights later, Madame simply left the master bedroom door ajar so that Louis could sneak in if he chose to do so. As he lay in the queen-sized bed, drowsing, Dalong could time almost exactly when Louis would leave his crate and picture his short fore and hind legs stretching to their utmost while climbing the long steps to the second floor, like when their son, Jimmy, was still a baby.

Back then they lived in a cramped efficiency and had to share a small kitchen and a malfunctioning bathroom in the narrow, dark hallway with two other families. How many times were unkind words exchanged between his wife and the women of the other families?

That was then and this was now.

When Jimmy—would Madame change their son's name to François or any other more regal-sounding French name?—came back for the weekend from the Summer English Camp, Louis greeted him at the door, wagging his tail happily, as if they had been friends for a long time.

"Wow, it's a poodle!" Jimmy exclaimed. "Ma, when did you get it? Why didn't you tell me? What's its name?"

Most of his friends, or their mothers, both at the camp and

at the elite New Century Boarding School, had pets now. Johnny's mother had a Golden Retriever, Tommy's a Rottweiler, Lisa's a large green-eyed, snow-white Persian cat. Seeing his son rolling on the floor with Louis, laughing joyously, Dalong smiled, too.

As the summer progressed, Dalong began to imagine seeing curly, harsh-textured hair on the family room's cherry hardwood floor, and on the light-colored carpet in the bedroom upstairs. He asked Mama Han to vacuum almost every day. But as long as everyone—excepting him, and Mama Han, perhaps—was happy, that was fine.

Every now and then he would even lend his hand in giving Louis a good bath, a major family event which would expect all hands available to pitch in, Mama Han filling the tub with warm water, Madame applying shampoo on Louis' furry body, Monsieur rinsing it off and in the process receiving a full face of soapy water when Louis, suddenly, spasm-like, shook from head to tail, and Jimmy drying up Louis with a large, fluffy towel.

Still Dalong couldn't get accustomed to having Louis around at night.

One night, while asleep, he turned in bed and felt something puffy, furry nestling next to him. By force of habit he reached out and gathered that thing in his arms, gently, and was rewarded with a big, wet lick in the face. He woke up and looked into the dark, smiling eyes of Louis. He let out a yell, threw Louis off of the bed, and sent him yelping out of the master bedroom, tail between his hind legs.

"What are you doing, you turtle's—" Madame jumped off of the bed after Louis.

The next day, Dalong ordered a king-sized bed to be delivered to his home. He could sleep in the guest room. It had a nice full-sized bed and some basic furniture. But what would Mama Han think? And he didn't want Jimmy to have wrong ideas about his dad and mom, either. Several of his classmates' parents had either separated or divorced because their dads had "little honeys" on the side.

From that day on Louis never slept in their bed again even though there was more than enough space for all three of them in the enormous new bed. Madame became increasingly tender and more attentive to Louis, fussing about his diet, his weight, his toenails, and the right style to trim the hair on his face, legs, and tail.

It was around this time, not long after National Day that Dalong acquired a "little honey" on the side, something that he had never dreamed would happen to him. He had never been exactly the morally self-righteous type who would condemn to hell his business partners and associates who indulged in indiscriminate amorous pursuits as if there were no tomorrow. He was simply too busy expanding his text messaging and online shopping services to waste his time and energies (and money, of course) on things he didn't really need.

As businesses expanded, he hired a new executive assistant, out of a pool of a couple of hundred applicants. A recent college graduate, Cindy appeared to be very confident, well organized, knowledgeable about the market, and quite competent with basic office technologies. She wasn't very pretty, though, but what did that matter?

The first morning Cindy came to work, he was busy looking for something in one of the messy file cabinets in his cluttered office.

"Freeze. Hands up!" A soft voice commanded from behind his back.

Startled, he whirled around and looked into the smiling eyes of his new executive assistant.

When did she come in?

"I'm sorry. Did I scare you, CEO Li?" She giggled, gaily, apologetically. There was a nice ringing quality in her voice, and a kind of girlish shyness beneath her apparent enthusiasm.

By the end of the day, everything in his office had been properly filed, labeled, and put in the right drawer in the right cabinet. His schedule for the next two full weeks had been organized and marked clearly on the big calendar on his executive desk. And with the addition of a bonsai, a vase of asparagus fern, and other in-house plants on the windowsills and atop the file cabinets, the office looked livelier.

Soon he began to rely on his capable executive assistant and took her along on business trips. When boisterous businessmen challenged her to another cup of strong liquor at the dinner table, he would become protective—"Don't you guys see her face is already red beyond recognition?"—which would invite loud, insinuating protests all around. Late at night, as he sat in his hotel room watching a bit of TV before going to bed, he would be conscious of her movement in the room next door, and the muffled sound of water gushing down from the showerhead.

One day, after closing a hard-bargained deal in Shanghai, they came back and settled in their separate hotel rooms. When he woke up, some time in the middle of the night, he heard a light, but persistent knock on the door.

"CEO Li, it's me. Cindy." He heard a soft, shivering voice.

He hurried out of bed and opened the door.

Still in pajamas, his executive assistant was hugging herself with her long arms, trembling badly.

"What happened? Come in!"

"I don't know," Cindy murmured through chattering teeth. "I'm cold . . . like I'm having malaria . . . sorry. . . CEO Li, perhaps I should go back to . . ."

"No, nonsense!" He put his hands on her young, shaking shoulders and led her to the edge of his bed. He felt her forehead.

"Oh, my, you've got a fever, burning hot!"

He fumbled in his bag and took out a few small bottles.

"Take two of these," he said, bringing a glass of water close to her mouth. "Tylenol Extra Strength. It should help."

Then he helped Cindy into his bed, went to her room next door to grab her bed cover and blanket, and spread them all on top of her.

"I'm still very cold." Her teeth chattered as she huddled into a small ball.

He crawled into bed and gathered the girl in his arms gently. Even though they were separated by the linen of their pajamas, he could feel the curves of her young body, her slender, smooth arms, and his warm breath on the nape of her neck. He didn't know when Cindy finally calmed down or when he dozed off close to morning.

Neither of them mentioned the incident afterwards. Cindy became doubly diligent in her work and more attentive to her boss, down to the kind of tea he drank and the kind of sleeping pills he took for occasional insomnia. She even became protective at dinner table when other loud businessmen tried to force another cup of strong liquor on CEO Li.

The next time they went on a business trip, he booked only one room at a four-star hotel. At the end of the long day, as they stepped into the hotel's elevator, Cindy placed her soft, quivering hand in his. He saw two faces in the mirror glowing with nervous expectancy.

It was the first time Dalong had ever muted his cell phone at night.

When Dalong came back from the two-day business trip, his wife noticed something different about him.

"What is it? Just back from your honeymoon or what?"

He attributed it to "the biggest merger ever" he had secured.

"No wonder," she murmured, and then asked, as if it were an afterthought, her eyes still fixed on his face: "That new assistant of yours. Did she go with you?"

Yes, but there was nothing she, Madame, should worry about concerning the assistant, he reassured. Madame had seen the girl, hadn't she? Though a full round of zodiac older, Madame would win, hands down, if there were a beauty contest between the two.

"Monsieur being bad today!" Madame, apparently pleased, turned to the poodle in her arms. "Right, Louis?"

Madame began to be more attentive to her makeup, her clothes, and the way she walked. She giggled more often and more heartily when she gossiped with her friends on the phone.

One day, she called while Dalong and his executive assistant were going over some contracts in the office. He ignored the persistent buzz on his cell phone.

"Don't you want to answer it?" Cindy reminded him.

He shook his head.

A few minutes later he received a text message from his wife:

"URGENT. CALL HOME RIGHT AWAY!"

When he called, he heard deep breathing at the other end, and the noise of someone licking the mouthpiece with a big, wet tongue.

"Call daddy," his wife cooed in the background.

"It's not funny." he muttered and hung up.

A few days after the phone call from Louis, Dalong tiptoed to his executive assistant's desk and dangled something in front of her face.

"I've got a gift for you, Cindy," he whispered.

"What is it?" Cindy looked up and her face blossomed like a red rose instantly. She grabbed the keys and gave him a long, juicy kiss.

That same day Cindy moved out of the apartment she had been sharing with another girl and moved into their new love nest.

From that day on Dalong began to come home much later, sometimes well past midnight. Business was expanding faster than he had anticipated, he mumbled apologetically one time as he slid into the king-sized bed. He was caught up in a cutthroat competition with another text messaging service provider, he explained another time.

One day, well past midnight, when he pushed open the master bedroom door, Dalong saw the enormously puffy, fluffy head of Louis on a pillow next to his wife. He lay down on his side of the bed as quietly as he could. Louis opened his eyes once, but didn't make any noise.

Then the unexpected happened. One day, after a night of sweet nonsense and wild abandonment to passions in their love nest, Dalong and his executive assistant were both exhausted and dozed off. When he woke up, it was already the next morning. There were several urgent text messages on his cell phone.

When they rushed back to the office, his wife was already waiting at the door, Louis by her side on a false diamond-studded leash. Madame looked tired. Her face didn't show the benefit of careful makeup. Her eyes, somewhat swollen, were fixed on him, then on his executive assistant.

"Bitch!" she grunted through her nose, turned abruptly, and left, Louis wobbling in tow.

Dalong came home much earlier that day. When he went upstairs after a quiet dinner and some TV, he found the master bedroom door locked from inside. He sighed and walked toward the guest room at the other end of the hallway, next to Jimmy's room.

Madame never raised a scene. They never talked about it. And he began to come home as early as before he had acquired a "little honey" on the side.

One day before dinner, he offered to feed Louis. When he reached to the plate next to the crate, Louis charged at his hand, like an enraged lion, displaying his sharp, white fangs. He would have been bitten if he hadn't withdrawn his hand in time.

"Little bastard!" he exclaimed angrily. Louis seemed as vicious as the large, famished dog that had bitten him when he was still a second grader back in his village. Every day when he walked the mud country road to school, Dalong would have to pass this thatched house where the dog was lurking in wait for him. It would growl ferociously when he was still quite some distance away and dart to meet him when he treaded closer, sniffing ravenously at his school bag which contained a corn pancake for lunch. One day, he got really scared and started to run. He tripped and felt something sharp being sunk deep into his butt.

That was why he didn't feel a bit of remorse for the dog when a few months later he saw its dead body sprawled atop a pile of other dead dogs on a two-wheeled barrow. The People's Commune's young militiamen, wearing red arm bands, sticks and ropes in hand, were annihilating all dogs in a frantic campaign to prevent a rumored rabies case from spreading into an epidemic. He wasn't sympathetic either when some old peasants, watching the loaded wheelbarrow parading out of the village, sighed deeply:

"Looks like we won't have bone-warming dog meat on snowy evenings this year!"

One evening, when he finally had a legitimate excuse to go home late again, Dalong dashed to the love nest he hadn't visited for some time. When the door was opened, he was met with a new, doggish face.

"Surprise!" His "little honey" giggled joyously.

It was a surprise indeed. Was there a conspiracy in this world that the women in his life had to have a dog, somehow?

He recovered quickly and managed a smile.

"You don't like dogs? Then I'll return—"

"I do." He grinned a bit more broadly.

Cindy's face flushed with joy again. It was a Chihuahua, she chattered. Why a Chihuahua? Because it was less pretentious than, say, the Golden Retriever, or the Poodle. The Chihuahua was every bit as energetic and outgoing as the other two, but somewhat shy underneath it all, very much like her.

That was the first time Dalong had stayed at their love nest without having a chance to abandon himself to pent-up passions. Cindy was so preoccupied with Huahua—a rather modest name for the puppy—the whole time. When they finally settled into the bedroom, he was so conscious of Huahua whimpering outside the door that he had difficulty concentrating.

Early spring the following year, Dalong heard a rumor that a few people in Guangdong had died of an unknown disease which had symptoms—high fever and severe headache—not unlike that of pneumonia. What was going on? He surfed on the Internet and paid more attention to the text messages flooding the cell phone panel: More people were dying of this mysterious disease each day; whole schools, hospitals, and neighborhoods in Guangdong, Beijing, and elsewhere were being quarantined; SARS—the official name for the strange, deadly respiratory disease—had jumped from some weird, monkey-like animals to humans thanks to Cantonese folks who ate them as delicacies. "Serve those Cantonese gluttons right!" He grunted through his nose.

Soon, even in his own city, thousands of miles away from the epicenters of the new terror, he began to see more and more faces covered with huge white gauze masks; faces, of which only the eyes could be seen, hurrying along busy streets, staring blankly outside the windows of crowded buses. Women in expensive leather jackets, their proud noses hidden underneath layers of white linen, would stop every now and then to check the masks their cute foreign puppies were wearing.

Madame's well-connected *majiang* friends gave her more than a dozen masks for Louis. With his mountainous head of puffy, fluffy fur, the Poodle looked hilarious with a mask on.

Cindy managed to obtain half a dozen masks for Huahua, too.

A businessman who had just returned from SARS-plagued Guangdong complained of a nagging fever and headache. The whole seven-story upscale residential building where his apartment was ended up being put under quarantine right away. For more than two weeks food and other basic daily supplies had to be packed in baskets and hoisted up to the 50-odd families through their windows by health care personnel in full protection gear.

Then word came that city authorities had decided to annihilate all pets—dogs, cats, whatever—as part of a frantic campaign to prevent SARS from escalating into a full-blown epidemic.

"Poor Louis. What should we do, Monsieur?" Madame sobbed, her eyes moistening.

"Poor Huahua. Where should we hide Huahua, Dalong?" Cindy held the puppy in her arms, teary-eyed.

He began to see expensive dogs and cats of all kinds wandering around in the streets without their proud owners, a wild, frightened look in their eyes.

Would it be okay if he took Louis and Huahua to Mama Han's home village in Anhui to wait until the crisis blew itself out?

Mama Han said yes.

But Madame and Jimmy didn't want to hear about it. Louis would be starved into a skinny monkey, they protested in chorus.

Cindy didn't want to part from Huahua for a single day,

either.

The next day, when he pulled into the gated residential compound, he saw a few grandpas and grannies from the Neighborhood Committee, all wearing red arm bands, leading uniformed public health officials knocking on the door of the first home near the gate, a van and a truck parked by the curbside.

He sped through the tree-lined road and slammed the car to a screeching stop when he reached home.

"They're coming!" He announced breathlessly when the door opened.

"Do something, please! Dalong!" His wife begged. There were tears in her voice.

"I've an idea!" He fumbled in his bag and took out a small bottle.

Between him and his wife they managed to force half a sleeping pill down Louis' throat. Then he gathered the puppy in his arms, gently. As he carried it upstairs to the master bedroom, his wife in tow, Louis nestled against his chest, like a baby, its shiny dark eyes on his face, its long, wet tongue licking his chin several times.

When he tucked the puppy in on the king-sized bed, his cell phone buzzed. He glanced at it, then at his wife, but didn't answer it.

"Have a nice sleep, kiddo," he patted the puppy on its furry cheeks, jokingly. "I . . . Daddy will be back soon."

His cell phone buzzed again, persistently.

He glanced at it. A new text message flashed:

"URGENT AS EYEBROWS ON FIRE! HUAHUA!"

He looked up and saw his wife's eyes on him.

"You do what you have to do, Dalong," she murmured

softly. "But don't forget the promise you've just made."

Dalong felt something warm rushing to his face, nodded, and dashed downstairs. As he sped away in his car, he saw the Pet Annihilation Team coming out of a home not too far from his, two uniformed public health officials carrying a chocolate-colored crate between them.

Buddha's Feet

He wasn't doing badly by anyone's standard.

As mayor of a five hundred plus household village, Fagui Chen had ample reasons to believe that he was doing exceptionally well. He wasn't the egg of a dragon or the son of a county's magistrate. Neither did he have the benefit of a college education. But look where he was now. Except for thumbing through newspapers and government instructional documents over a cup of freshly made tea in his office, being the honored guest at feasts for both Red and White Happiness events, or once in a long while traveling to the county for meetings and policy study sessions, Mayor Chen spent most of his time "laying the bricks for the Great Wall" with other village officials at the *majiang* table in his office or at home, a small, simple two-story brick and cement thing, the grandest in the whole of Chen Village.

Nevertheless, Fagui hadn't been very happy lately. The freshly made Dragon Well tea didn't taste as refreshing as before. Tender, juicy roasted piglets didn't bite as appetizing. And he would wake up in the middle of the night, stare at the ceiling blankly, and sigh.

"What is it?" his wife, Meirong, mumbled in the darkness.

He sighed again and turned to face the wall. What's the use explaining it to a woman who wouldn't be able to comprehend?

Besides, the mayor, a thin but rigorous man of small stature, had become less patient with his wife who had been sapped quite a bit after giving birth to a precious son at the age of 35.

A few weeks ago Fagui had gone to the county for a meeting, the first to be held in the newly-constructed County Government Compound. When he arrived in the village's old truck, his eyes were dazzled by what was looming right in front of him: the thirty-*mu* gated compound—with its shiny, glassy ten-floor main building right in the center, a big gurgling water fountain surrounded by exotic plants and flowers and little pebble paths winding through lush green, well-manicured lawns, and black and white brand new cars parked neatly on either side—basking in the brilliant morning sunshine.

Was he having a vision? Was he at the gate of Heaven itself? For the whole day, Fagui was drifting from the grand, velvety auditorium to fluffily-carpeted conference rooms to the stainless steel cafeteria in a tipsy, dazed state of mind. When late in the afternoon he finally sat down again next to Young Zhao who came to pick up the mayor in his beat-up truck, loaded with bags of seed and fertilizer, Fagui could hardly tear his eyes away from the compound shimmering in the dizzying glory of the sinking sun.

What's that saying? Fagui wondered as the truck bumped along the narrow country road home to Chen Village. One would rather be the head of a small chicken than the tail of a huge cow? What nonsense!

If nothing else, Fagui knew what he wanted and once he wanted something, he knew how to get it. That was how years back, when he was still a young bumpkin with no particular talent, no looks, no promising prospect of a future, he won the hand of the daughter of a powerful, well-respected mayor, and how he climbed into the fiercely-contested, lucrative chair of mayoralty years later.

That day at the new County Government Compound was a rude awakening for Fagui. He began to travel to the county much more frequently to report work to the heads of its various departments and offices. He was respectful, sincere, and thorough. He would nod religiously or grin heartily whenever the head of a department or office had said something he deemed witty. When it was time for him to leave, Fagui would open his briefcase, in a way that would suggest that the act was no more than an afterthought, and produce a small red envelope stuffed with ten Great Unity bills, his eyes beaming with smile:

A small token from the hearts of the people of the Chen Village, hahaha!

Of all the departmental heads, Fagui was particularly taken with Old Ba, Director of the powerful Personnel Department. That was where the mayor of Chen Village would linger a bit longer, nod a bit more earnestly, and the red envelopes he left on the table became quite a bit more bulging. Old Ba seemed to be favorably impressed with Fagui, too. He would even bother to come out from behind his large executive desk and see Fagui to the door.

"Young Chen," Old Ba would say, holding his right hand and patting him on the left shoulder, warmly, "I've heard good things about you. Keep working hard so we in the county won't be disappointed."

Three months after launching the quiet campaign, Fagui heard on the grapevine that he was being considered for the position of Deputy Director of the Office of Rural Industries, whose responsibility was to supervise, support, and promote the county's several hundred small paper mills, handcraft shops, and other profitable and not so profitable enterprises run by the villages.

He was told by a reliable source from the county that the competition was keen. The mayor of another village, Yang, was a top candidate, too. Though neither a dragon's egg nor a county magistrate's son, either, Fagui's rival had three years of post-secondary school education, was younger, more energetic, and just as well liked by the heads of the county's various departments and offices. His village's mills and shops had been the envy of the whole county, too.

Once again Fagui stayed wide-eyed in bed and stared at the ceiling well past midnight, sighing profusely. He knew that now that he had already hit forty, this would be his last shot at anything bigger than Chen Village.

"Perhaps you should go and burn a few incense sticks at the temple," his wife murmured by his side in the darkness. "The one on Green Dragon Hill, you know."

Fagui was irritated by the suggestion though he didn't bother to say anything: What superstition! What do you take me for? I'm Mayor Chen, who has benefited from studying newspapers and government documents for so many years! Besides, that would mean, literally, clasping Buddha's feet at the last minute.

"You think I could've got pregnant with Bao Bao, after two girls in a row," Meirong muttered, as if she had read his mind, "if I hadn't climbed up there and burned incense sticks and made some offerings?" She yawned and turned, her sleepy voice dwindling into a mosquito-like buzz.

A few days later, Fagui rolled out of bed before the first crow of roosters, took a bath, put on his best clothes, and embarked on a pilgrimage to the temple on Green Dragon Hill about half an hour walk to the west of Chen Village.

As he was halfway up the narrow, stony path on Green Dragon Hill, the billowing early morning fog was beginning to dissolve. Fagui paused to look around. He couldn't see anything clearly, but had a vague sense of the world out there—including his Chen Village—stirring up to a new day with new promises.

Soon he could make out the temple perched precariously at the tip of the hill. Beyond the temple was vast, endless sky cheered by the first flush of morning. It was at this time that Fagui was hit with an eerie feeling of having been there before, in another life of his, perhaps. Was this one of those déjà vu phenomena he had read about in the newspapers?

The temple was a small, simple wooden thing, smaller, simpler, and lower than Fagui's residence. The stairway leading up to the door was narrow and short. The poles, the rails, and the walls, having seen years and years of relentless rain and wind, looked blistered. And its roof, steep, A-shaped, with weather-beaten dark shingles, was nothing like those spectacular octagonal or double, upturn-eaved roofs he had seen on TV.

The door was already open. It was still somewhat dim inside. As he stepped in, a faintly familiar air greeted his nostrils. The fragrance smelt unearthly and a bit nauseating.

His eyes adjusted quickly. Sitting right in front of him, in the center of the temple, bare-footed, cross-legged, was a figure about Fagui's height. The figure's face was chubby, his eyes kind, calm, almost beaming, but penetrating, as if he had already known the visitor for a long, long time.

With trembling fingers, Fagui placed a pair of incense sticks into the burner, lit them, and fell on his knees.

He didn't know how to pray or ask for blessings. His mind was being filled with so many earthly things. Laying bricks for the Great Wall in his office. The first time he had his way with Meirong in the cornfields—oh, she was such a young and pretty thing back then! Callus-less, womanly hands of Old Ba resting in his own. Bao Bao—the kid could already read more than one hundred characters and do simple addition now! Mouthwatering aroma from whole piglets roasted golden brown. Small, wrinkled red envelopes folks of Chen Village pulled out of their inner pockets with quivering hands. Fat red envelopes he left on the desks of county officials. The office for Deputy Director of the Office of Rural Industries—smaller than that for the Director, crowded with messy, old cabinets. The thirty-*mu* gated County Government Compound glittering under a blazing sun. Mayor Yang—

A not so kind, not so generous thought occurred to him in association with his younger and more energetic rival. Fagui was annoyed with himself for having thought the thought at this time and at this place of all places. Sheepishly, he raised his head. The figure in front of him was still gazing down at him with the same kind, calm, yet penetrating eyes. Not another soul was around. Fagui let out an inaudible sigh and lowered his eyes.

He noticed something odd with the figure in front of him.

Something missing.

The big toe of Buddha's right foot.

Fagui broke into a cold sweat as it all came rushing back to him.

He had been inside this temple before. As a small kid. A

first or second grader, perhaps. Tagging behind a gang of loud, block-headed young bumpkins on a moonlit evening, all wearing Red Guard armbands and carrying bricks or sticks. They were here to demolish the temple and smash the Buddha statue to pieces in a frenzied campaign to rid the world of all the superstitious and poisonous relics from the old society.

For a while the temple was being filled with things crashing to the floor and the young rebels' crazed laughs.

All of a sudden, from behind the battered statue came a deep, thunderous, enraged howl as if from the depths of another, ageless world. Terrified, the young rebels took to their feet. They never dared to come back and finish the work.

Why on earth have I forgotten this little incident in my early life all these years? Fagui wondered. Was it because the violent, fitful fever I suffered for days afterward had burnt a hole in my memory?

Fagui was now more than angry with Meirong—"Woman!"—for having suggested this incense-burning idea and with himself for having fallen to it. More than anything else, he was stung by what he perceived to be the ultimate injustice of it all: of all the damages that had been wrecked by the young rebels more than thirty years ago, only his, the most harmless of all, perhaps, remained unrepaired to this day.

He stole a glance around. Still not a soul nearby. He inched forward on his knees and touched—there was no way he could clasp Buddha's feet, the way the Lord was sitting—where the big toe should have been. It felt rugged and cold. Would Buddha forgive me, not to say bless me, and grant me my wishes?

He heard soft footsteps and rustling of clothing.

"Amituofo," a deep, ancient voice intoned by his side. It

sounded eerily familiar, too

Startled, Fagui turned and looked into the face of someone wrapped in a long, yellow robe. With his leathery skin and bushy, frosty eyebrows, the monk, still chanting in his deep voice, looked as ancient as the temple itself.

"Amituofo," Fagui found his voice and mumbled after the monk, all the while being irritated by the cold dampness between his skin and the well-starched new shirt.

An eternity had passed before Fagui inched backward on his knees to have a respectful distance from Buddha and kowtowed three times, his forehead touching the hard floor each time.

Still flustering with nervous excitement, Fagui got on his feet, placed a stuffed red envelope on the altar, and staggered out of the temple.

When a dazed Fagui hurried downhill along the narrow, stony path, the fog had completely dissipated. The world around the hill, between a cloudless, steel-blue sky and the endless fields on earth, was flooded with brilliant, giddying sunshine.

That same day Fagui took another trip to the county to report work to the heads of various departments and offices, his briefcase filled with red envelopes stuffed with Great Unity bills. When Old Ba saw him to the door of his office, the Director of Personnel Department grasped Fagui's hand and patted him on the shoulder more earnestly than ever:

"Young Chen, don't you lose much sleep over this. We in the county will follow the guidelines and proper procedures strictly and choose the best, the most qualified to fill the position. Trust us."

A week later, Fagui heard through the grapevine that Mayor

Yang's candidacy was in serious trouble because the Personnel Department had received letters accusing him of embezzlement of public funds and an immoral, corrupt lifestyle.

"Turtle's son!" Fagui muttered through clenched teeth. "I knew he's a bad egg!"

From then on, things began to move fast. Two weeks after the rumor concerning his rival's candidacy, Fagui traveled to the county, suit and tie and leather shoes—all shiny and uncomfortably new—to report to work. As he sat down behind the desk in the crowded office for the Deputy Director of the Office of Rural Industries in the County Government Compound, Fagui was more than glad that he had listened to his wife and taken the trip to Green Dragon Hill.

Deputy Director Chen worked diligently. If nothing else, Fagui was a quick learner. In a few short months, he knew exactly where all the official seals were and got the hang of how to execute his official duties. He remained every bit as respectful and sincere as before when he talked to the heads of the other departments and offices, nodded thoughtfully or smiled heartily whenever they said something he deemed weighty. He even had a chance to go to the office of the County Magistrate to make a report on work. It was a real eye-popping experience. The Magistrate's office was a spectacular suite, with a pretty, young secretary manning the front desk, the Magistrate himself sitting behind a huge, deep-colored executive desk, two huge floor-length windows, several soft-cushioned chairs and a burgundy genuine leather couch for visitors, elegant bonsai in expensive pots, long, bold calligraphy scrolls on the wall, and a side door leading to a large conference room.

Fagui was blushingly conscious of the fact that he might indeed be the tail of a huge cow in this enormous compound. Yet when he rode in a government car to the villages to check how their mills and shops were doing, Deputy Director Chen was always received as a real big shot. He was wined and dined and presented—"It's from the hearts of the people of our whole village!"—with so many stuffed red envelopes that he had to use an alias and PINs to establish several new bank accounts.

By the end of the year, Fagui had demolished the old brick and cement house of his and built a brand new residence fit for someone of his status: a two-*mu* gated compound with a red-roofed, stucco-walled building filled with fluffy carpet, soft-cushioned chairs, a genuine leather couch, a big screen Sony TV set and much more, the grandest in the whole of Chen Village and kilometers beyond. He had gotten rounder, too, and his belly now looked more like that of Lord Buddha. Meirong, the two girls, Bao Bao—oh, nothing in the whole universe could fill his heart with more joy than watching the kid playing Nintendo on the big screen—and just about everyone in the Chen clan were so thrilled with his sudden, good fortune.

And good fortune never came singly. So that Deputy Director Chen could better serve the people and execute his official duties, the county decided to provide him with a two-bedroom apartment in a new residential complex built exclusively for the benefit of the county officials. That way Fagui didn't have to commute daily between Chen Village and the small, but vibrant city, the seat of the county government. Now he had time to go swimming—dog paddle—in the Olympic-size pool in the complex or to run around, gasping, trying to catch the ball with his racquet on the tennis court. What he really enjoyed doing, though, was going to fancy restaurants and karaoke halls to talk over work with associates and to treat officials from the province's Bureau of Rural Industries. He even found time to lay the bricks for the Great Wall at *majiang* tables again with his new friends.

Sometimes when he woke up in the middle of the night in his new apartment and felt the warm, supple body of a half-naked young waitress or a beauty salon masseuse nestling against his fleshy, egg-shaped mass, Fagui would be amazed by how far he had come in such a short time. What's wrong with being the tail of a big, fat, golden cow? He mused. It's a thousand times more delicious than being the head of a small, scrawny chicken. Besides, he, Fagui, wasn't really the smallest, the most inconsequential in the County Government Compound anyway. That honor had to go to the numerous secretaries, assistants, and yes, even janitors busying themselves with their errands all the time.

Even though he wasn't sure how much he owed his sudden good fortune to his visit to Green Dragon Hill, Fagui didn't want to err on the side of being perceived as not knowing how to express his gratitude. Therefore, the first thing he did, when just about everything else had been taken care of, was to make another trip to Green Dragon Hill.

Dawn had not yet broken when he finally reached the top of the hill. The world below and all around was still drowsing in a blurring mist. Yet there was already a sizable crowd waiting; everybody wanted to be the very first to place incense sticks in the burner and make their offerings.

"Told you to get up an hour earlier," Meirong, who was accompanying her husband this time, murmured by his side.

"Just about everybody knows how you were blessed by. . . ."

Woman! Fagui thought to himself. He could picture Meirong broadcasting his good fortune, in a most confidential tone, to the whole village. Gratified as he was by the admiring, envious glances everybody was casting in his direction, Fagui was annoyed that now he had to share the secret of success with the whole of Chen Village and beyond.

The old monk had become too old and had since retired to a place nobody knew. The thirtyish new monk's face glowed with good health. His gaze was warm and direct. His movement was brisk, displaying such a sense of purpose and confidence that, if it hadn't been for his shaved head and the long, yellow robe, nobody would have taken him for a monk. While kowtowing on his knees, murmuring "Amitoufo," Fagui heard a faint buzz from the person of the monk who was chanting just two or three meters from him. The monk needs a cell phone to communicate with Lord Buddha himself?

When the service was over, Deputy Director Chen took the monk aside from the multitude and introduced himself.

"Amitoufo," Monk the Enlightened beamed warmly. "I've heard about you from Monk the Infinite Kindness."

"What did he say?" Fagui asked anxiously.

"That," the new monk winked, knowingly, "I'm not at liberty to disclose."

Glancing around them quickly, Fagui took from his pocket an envelope twice as big as the one he had presented a year ago.

"I want to give this to you directly instead of leaving it on the altar. I have been thinking," Fagui paused, watching the monk's face closely. "I've been thinking that it's about time we renovated this temple to catch up with the times."

"I have to confess," Monk the Enlightened bowed his shaved head, "that I've been thinking about the very same for some time. But, as you well know, it would depend on the kindness of the folks around here, and more than anything else, the big-hearted kindness of a patron like you."

"Nothing gives me more joy," Fagui faltered, almost blushing, "than having a chance to do what a dutiful public servant is supposed to do, you know."

"Amitoufo," Monk the Enlightened bowed again, then spoke slowly and deliberately. "The first glance I had of you, in the multitude waiting at the door, the shape of your forehead, your nose, your chin, everything about you, I knew right away that you are someone special, someone who will bring glory to this place (Fagui glowed inside), whose destiny is bigger than the villages around here (Already a proven fact!), bigger than the whole county (Fagui had dreamed of one day dropping the word "Deputy" from his title. If coaxed or coerced with more effective means, he would confess that he even dreamed of—only once—thumbing through newspapers and government documents behind that huge, shiny, deep-colored executive desk in the Magistrate's office suite), and probably bigger than the province . . . ."

Fagui had been to the Province Government Compound, ten times larger and grander than his county's, with armed guards manning the gate. . . . What can I, Fagui, do there? Being Deputy Director of the Bureau of Rural Industries? Lieutenant Governor? Governor? And beyond the province? Even if I had swallowed leopard's bile whole, I would not dare to dream that far!

Yet this was what he had heard from Monk the Enlightened himself.

Perhaps. Perhaps he, Fagui, was a dragon's egg after all, even though he hadn't known it all his life?

Now that he knew his real destiny, though he wasn't a hundred percent sure of it, Fagui started to work on it right away. He had his assistant draft a proposal to completely renovate the temple on Green Dragon Hill as a cultural site, and a tourism spot, so that it would better meet the spiritual needs of the common people in the surrounding area.

After many visits to the various departments and offices and even an audience with the County Magistrate himself, Deputy Director Chen was able to secure enough funds for the construction of a brand new temple, twice the size of the old one, with a much broader and longer stairway leading to the entrance, and an upturned, double-eaved roof.

Within the month, a busy, beaming Fagui accompanied the Magistrate and many other county officials to attend the groundbreaking ceremony—a grand fanfare which attracted a couple of hundred people—before construction started. It was the crowning moment in his entire forty some years of life so far and the harbinger of greater, more dazzling glory showered over his head.

Two days later, he was told that when construction workers lifted the old Buddha from his seat—oh, it had taken a whole bunch of them with levers, pry bars, and ropes—they found a broken toe underneath the statue, and that a young worker, who had pocketed the toe as a souvenir, fell off the roof and broke his neck when they were demolishing the old temple.

"They say," Meirong woke him up in the middle of the night, "perhaps Lord Buddha isn't too happy about this idea of building a new home for Him."

"Superstition!" Fagui grunted through his nose. "Who on earth doesn't want a newer, bigger, and grander residence?"

Nevertheless, Fagui was nervous for quite a few days. He was extremely careful and watched every step he took wherever he went. Yet the construction went ahead without any more accidents. Even the rumor that a team from the province would soon come down to investigate charges of rampant bribery and decadent lifestyle among the county officials had died down. Fagui breathed with relief and resumed his dream of a future beyond the county, and beyond the province, perhaps.

Three months later, a brand new temple, golden, arching, magnificent, appeared on the tip of Green Dragon Hill. The old stony, narrow footpath had also been replaced with a new asphalt road wide enough for two cars.

The evening before the grand opening ceremony, Fagui took his family to the new temple to burn incense sticks, make offerings, and ask for blessings. Monk the Enlightened granted him the privilege of being the very first to do so thanks to his special contributions to the temple.

"Amitoufo," Fagui murmured earnestly as he knelt down in front of the new standing Buddha stature made of copper plated with shiny gold. At least twice as high and thick as his sitting predecessor, Lord Buddha looked at Fagui and his family with the same kind, calm, almost beaming, but penetrating eyes.

Fagui inched forward on his knees, his egg-shaped belly brushing the cold, hardwood floor—"Pa looks so funny! So stupid!" He heard Bao Bao laughing aloud mirthfully from behind—and encircled his arms around Buddha's feet, clasped them tightly, and rested his face against their cold, metallic surface.

He could already see himself signing on documents behind the big executive desk in the Magistrate's grand office suite. . . .

His cell phone buzzed. Damn it. I should've turned it off.

One arm still clasping Buddha's feet, Fagui fished out the phone from his pocket.

"Comrade Fagui Chen," he heard Old Ba at the other end. "The investigation team from the province will arrive tomorrow morning." Fagui's head swirled. "The Magistrate has instructed that assisting the team's work will be the top priority for the next few weeks or months." Old Ba coughed, then continued. "Therefore, all other work and activities, including the grand opening ceremony for the new temple on Green Dragon Hill, have to be postponed indefinitely. . . ."

Fagui couldn't believe his ears. But that was exactly what he had heard. Old Ba told him to hurry back to the County Government Compound so that they could strategize together how they could best assist the investigation team's work.

He released the other arm from around Buddha's feet, stood up breathlessly, and hurried out of the temple, ignoring the "Amitoufos" flowing from the murmuring lips of Monk the Enlightened.

"I haven't clasped Buddha's feet yet!" Bao Bao whined behind him. "I don't want to go home yet. I want to clasp Buddha's feet, too!"

Fagui whirled and gave his son a dirty stare.

"Be quiet," Meirong picked up Bao Bao in her arms and whispered to his ears, but loud enough for Fagui to hear. "Pa's busy. . . we can always come back. . . just you and me. . . ."

Fagui's chauffeur, who had been waiting in the small parking lot by the new temple, opened the door for everyone to get back in the car.

It was a moonless evening. The visibility was so limited that even with the high beams on Fagui couldn't have more than a blurry sense of the dusky world drowsing around and beyond Green Dragon Hill.

Everybody in the car remained dead quiet as the car hummed cautiously down the winding road toward the bottom of the hill. Nobody, not even Bao Bao sitting in Pa's lap, made a sound.

I should've had the foresight not to listen to Meirong, a befuddled Fagui regretted indignantly. Woman!

How Was Your Dance Today?

The living room was throbbing with aroma from the kitchen. Something was being poured into hot oil. It sizzled. A metal spatula stirred and turned whatever was sizzling in the wok continuously. The exhaust fan buzzed and whirred.

After changing into a pair of slippers placed near the door, he shuffled into the bathroom, washed his hands, his face, and checked himself in the mirror above the sink. The pupils underneath the bushy eyebrows looked like thickening mist on a snowy evening, but a tinge of late autumn sky would assert itself if anyone cared to gaze at them a bit more strenuously.

He nudged the kitchen door open with an index finger.

She had just poured a bowl of water into the empty wok on the two-burner gas stove. A white cloud was still mushrooming into the exhaust fan.

She shut off the fan.

The kitchen fell into a hushed, expansive silence.

He picked up the steamy plate on the narrow, white-tiled counter. It was a dish of red pepper, dry tofu, and pork, all finely sliced, stir-fried with green onion, ginger, and soy sauce.

Already on the table in the small dining room were an earthenware pot and an oval plate of steamed silvery butterfish.

He took out two sets of bowls, chopsticks, and soupspoons

from the cupboard, and laid them on the table.

She came in and removed the floral-patterned apron.

They sat down to eat.

The earthenware pot brimmed with a soup of spareribs and chopped baby bamboo shoots, fresh mushroom, and winter melon.

He dipped his spoon into the pot, got a spoonful of broth, and tasted tentatively. A string of staccato, watery "Ah! Ah! Ah!" escaped his lips as he reached for another spoonful.

She filled his bowl with shiny, well-cooked rice. The characters "Ten Thousand Years and Counting" in elegant calligraphic strokes glittered on the outside of the bowl.

He selected a slice from the butterfish's belly, caught it between the tips of his chopsticks, its tender meat quivering, and brought it to his mouth. While his tongue was still busy with the slice in his mouth, his chopsticks were already working on another piece from the fish's belly.

She dipped the tip of her spoon into the earthenware pot, sipped some broth, switched to chopsticks, picked up a morsel of this or that, and chewed deliberately.

A few minutes later, the stir-fry and the soup were almost half way down. All that was left of one side of the fish were long, sword-like bones.

He got hold of the fish between his soupspoon and chopsticks, turned it over, selected a slice of tender meat from its still intact side of the belly, and carried it in the direction of her bowl.

Seeing it coming, she covered her bowel with both hands. A few drops of deep-colored sauce fell on the backs of her hands.

Forced to change its course in midair, he turned the morsel

away sharply, made a half circle, and put it in his own bowl.

"How was your dance today?" she murmured, switching back to her spoon.

"Great," he mumbled, his tongue busy with the rejected slice of tender fish.

"Dancing is good for you."

"I know."

"That's what Dr. Liu said."

"Yeah." He chewed with relish.

"Good for your blood pressure."

"That's what the man said."

"Good for your weight."

"Well, I've lost quite a few *jin*, you know."

"Good for your heart."

"I know." He washed down the food in his mouth with a spoonful of broth.

"Yeah, it's good for you."

"Well?" He looked up from his bowl, and turned his eyes outside the window.

Cicadas were singing loudly in the deep green foliage of the poplars in the quad bathed in the dissipating glory of the early evening sun. Withered leaves, discarded shirts, and other dirty rags were scattered on the cement roof of the old two-story apartment building neighboring the new high-rise they had moved into only a year ago.

He turned his gaze back to his food.

A few more hearty mouthfuls later, he had advanced to the bottom of his bowl.

"So, how *was* the dance today?" She was still gazing outside the window.

"Told you it was great." He shook out a toothpick from a small bottle on the table.

"You did."

"Yeah?"

"How was *she* at the dance?"

"Who?" The toothpick stopped moving in the crack between the second and the third upper teeth.

"You know."

"Oh."

"How was she at the dance today?"

"You know." The toothpick resumed its movement between the teeth.

"I don't."

"You saw her dance before."

"Still good at kicking her leg high in the air and dropping into her partner's arms at the end of a tango?" She sounded genuinely concerned.

"Yeah, well—"

"Still good at swinging her hips this way and that way when fox-trotting, or just plain walking on the dance floor?"

He let the used toothpick drop into his emptied bowl.

"Why did they let a fiftyish kindergarten teacher retire?" There was innocent curiosity in her voice.

He shrugged. The expression "Beats me" was on his face.

"So that she could go to the Home of Retired Cadres to kick her long legs and swing her cute little hips everyday?" Her eyebrows knitted as if she was making an effort to puzzle out something. "Your old heart has broken down a few times before. It can't take that kind of kicking and swinging without breaking down again any time soon, you know that."

"Dr. Liu said—"

"Dr. Liu doesn't know crap."

He stood up, shuffled to the bedroom, and adjusted the window unit to "Cooler" and its fan to "Stronger." It groaned, choked, recovered, and hummed evenly again.

His shower was long and elaborate.

When he came out of the bathroom in cool clean clothes, he saw her huddling in a corner of the couch in the sitting room, her eyes on the TV screen without even a blink. The show was *Sunset Glories*.

He lumped down in the shiny bamboo lounge, fished out a small stool from underneath the lounge with his feet, extended his legs as far as he could, released the stool on the floor, and rested his feet on it comfortably.

When she got up and started walking to the bedroom, his feet grabbed the stool and withdrew it close to the lounge to give her room to pass.

Upon hearing water splashing in the bathroom, he picked up the remote on the coffee table and changed the program to *Be Happy*, an evening drama series he had been following.

He sighed, laughed, and slurped from the cup of cool green tea on the coffee table.

A short while later, she came back, her hair still wet, and resumed her seat in the corner of the couch.

They watched the drama together, quietly.

"So, she is still good at dancing." It sounded like a statement, an afterthought.

He kept his eyes on the screen.

They continued to watch *Be Happy*.

"Sufeng called." She said.

"She did? When?" A tinge of late autumn sky must be glimmering in his eyes.

"Right before you came back."

"What did she say? Is everything all right?"

"Yeah."

"Good."

"I talked to Jimmy, too." There was a faint glitter in her eyes.

"That kid! Told you that kid will amount to something."

A pause.

"Sufeng said dancing would be good for me, too." The light in her eyes flickered.

"She did?" The dull mist in his eyes must have reasserted itself.

"Being locked up here everyday would only kill me before my time, she said."

"You could come down, now and then, and take a walk—"

"That'd make a certain former kindergarten teacher really happy."

"—anytime you like, you know that."

"Just waltz and slower dance like that, you know, Sufeng said."

He continued to stare at the screen.

"But Dr. Liu said—" he murmured.

"Dr. Liu be damned!"

She was still in the corner of the couch when he came back from the bathroom, a little statue molded out of thin air.

The host of *Sunset Glories* was explaining "Three Proven Secrets of Longevity:" an upbeat attitude and equilibrium no matter what, a regular exercise program such as *taiji* or dancing, and . . . .

She stood up and started toward the bedroom. His feet grabbed the small stool soon enough to let her pass through.

He changed back to *Be Happy*, and slouched more deeply in the lounge, his feet resting on the small stool.

When the show was finally over, he flipped through the channels, and then pressed a red button on the remote. The TV flashed briefly and went dark. Only the refrigerator in the dining room continued its low, slow humming.

He got up and pushed open the bedroom door with an index finger and tiptoed in.

A flood of silvery moonlight poured in through the tall window and shone on her small, thin body on her side of the bed.

He lay down gingerly.

She stirred and breathed evenly again.

The air conditioner droned drowsily.

His eyes wandered on the wall beyond the bed and rested on a yellowed black and white photo in a large classic-colored wood frame.

The young woman in the photo was balanced on the tips of her toes, her snow-white short skirt in full bloom, her slender arms arching elegantly above her head. Her big, liquid eyes underneath long eyelashes, downcast, looked pensive.

He yawned inaudibly. He was ready to drift off to sleep.

"Will you take me to dance tomorrow?" It was a slow, almost inaudible murmur.

He was startled.

"What?"

"Take me to dance tomorrow."

The request, somewhat firmer, was still no more than a flimsy whisper.

"You want to?"

"Mmmm."

The sigh lingered in the air for a second or two and vanished.

"Okay."

The moonlit night dwindled into languid, drowsing silence.

He yawned a few more times and snored.

The Swallow: Not Exactly an Interlude

They always come back in spring.

The same pair of swallows.

They come back when the mid-March air still shudders with chills before the sun rises. When the long, cascading limbs of willows along the Twin-Sun River begin to shoot tender yellow, the peach trees in front of my home are alive with buds on their young, purplish twigs, and the sea of baby wheat far and beyond turns a vibrant green and its dewy blades glitter under the early morning sunshine.

I can feel them coming, sitting on the stone threshold of my home, both the front and back doors wide open, waiting.

I hear the swallows coming, chirping from far and high across the sea of rich green as the rising sun melts away the chills in my preadolescent body clad in a hand-me-down cotton-padded jacket.

Soon I catch glimpses of them, a whirling blur of shiny blue-black, clean white, and streaks of vivid red—tiny, silk strings that were tied to the birds' little feet the autumn before—as they appear in the sun-bathed sky, overtaking each other while diving precipitously only to soar again, painting dizzy circles and curves around my home, warbling all the while.

Then, they dart inside my home from the front door, a

startling rush of air over my head; they float on their sharply angled wings under the vaulted roof of beams and reeds; they chase each other up and down and left and right at unpredictable speeds; they perch tentatively on the beams, their long, forked tails quivering nervously, only to dart out of my home from the back door, a resonance of colors.

They weave in and out of my home for several more rounds before settling on a beam of the arched roof, the same song gushing from their bronzing throats, now in duet, now in chorus:

No borrowing of your charcoal,
No borrowing of your rice,
Only borrowing your home
To give birth to our babies.

Pa says that's what the swallows sing. They are good birds bringing luck to whoever's home they choose to stay in during the warm months from spring to autumn. Pa, principal of a rural middle school, knows.

The swallows start to build a new nest right away: a piece of straw, a small twig, a tiny clod of sticky earth at a time, which they pick up somewhere and hold in their beaks and dip in the cool water as they flit across the surface of the Twin-Sun River and carry home to place on the chosen beam, layer upon layer, with perfect alignment.

Within days a sturdy, tightly knit, rice bowl-shaped nest appears on the beam.

At the end of the day, when the sun has disappeared below the horizon in the west, my family—Pa, Ma, me, and my baby sister—gather around the faded dining table in the main room for supper, the swallows roosting in their nest overhead, crooning now and then.

"How's the new classroom building going?" Ma asks.

"Oh, great!" Pa looks up from his bowl, the wrinkled sleeves of his jacket studded with mud stains of amazing shapes and patterns. "We just need to make a thousand more mud-bricks and then we'll be fine."

When the willows have canopied the Twin-Sun River in rich green, the cloud of pink blossoms in front of my home have yielded to clusters of tiny peaches, and the sea of wheat, now taller than my belly button, murmurs and nods its sprouting heads in the warm breeze of early summer, five or six newly-hatched bundles of joy, snuggling one next to another, peek from behind the nest on the beam.

Whenever the Pa or Ma swallow comes home with a fat insect in its beak, their babies, one and all, open their soft yellow-edged mouths so wide, crying "Feed me!" "Feed me!" all at the same time, and I can see their mouths' pinkish interiors even from outside the front door.

The Pa or Ma swallow thrusts the meaty delicacy into a wide-open mouth and leaves home right away to catch another worm or dragonfly for the next wide-open mouth crying to be fed.

Pa picks up another pupil's essay from a pile on the small dining table placed near the front door, reads, chuckles, the tip of his fountain pen whisking on the margin every now and then, his puffy, prematurely-grayed hair glistening in the early Sunday morning sunlight.

Once, one of the baby swallows fell from the nest. When I

gently picked it up from the earthen floor, I could see the thin blue veins under its translucent skin where the soft feathers didn't cover completely. I climbed up the tall ladder Pa brought in to place the bird back into its home. Its siblings looked overjoyed to have their fallen brother or sister back, but not so pleased to see the face of a giant visitor so close.

By early autumn, when the Twin-Sun River is laced by the rusty foliage of willows, the golden peaches and wheat have long been harvested, and in front of my home now ripples a sea of deep green rice which already reaches where my belly button is, the baby swallows are ready to test their wings.

Cheered and escorted by their Pa and Ma, one by one, they emerge from the nest, leap into the air, and flutter out from the front or back door, carving faltering yet increasingly confident circles around my home, chirping all the while:

No borrowing of your charcoal,
No borrowing of your rice,
Only borrowing your home
To give birth to our babies.

Soon they soar and disappear into the velvety sky.

Not long after that, when the air chills again and I have to put on a warmer jacket, the Pa and Ma swallows leave, too. The world under the vaulted roof feels so quiet and so empty once more.

But they always come back in spring.

Except for the spring of 1966.

I was nine years old then. Only one of the pair returned,

the tiny silk string of vivid red still tied to its little foot.

Papa didn't say anything, but I knew that it was not an auspicious sign.

Red Guard Fantasies

Cuicui was checking her makeup with a small vanity, applying a stick of moisturizer along the natural line of her lips. They looked fuller, shinier, and more sensuous.

Even without the rearview mirror, Piao could picture her in his mind: pale skin, rich, lustrous hair, crescent eyebrows above a pair of liquid, almond eyes, a small, cherry mouth beneath the pointed nose, a long, ivory neck graced by a flimsy gold necklace with a glittering diamond-studded heart, a pair of white jade bracelets dangling on the thin wrists of lithe, smooth arms. . . .

He even knew how she smelled: just a hint of perfume, which would linger in his mind, like some vaguely-worded proposition, or an elusive, tantalizing thought he had been pursuing.

The only defect—if it would matter—was that her legs were a bit short, a few centimeters shy of being in perfect proportion to her upper body. And lately, a few lines seemed to have asserted themselves around the corners of her eyes. Otherwise, she could pass for a movie starlet—like. . .who?

"Old Piao, let's make a stop at the New Century Pla-za," Cuicui said, as the countdown in the traffic light blinking in the late summer afternoon sun was about to change to green. "I want to have a look and so some shop-ping."

Piao couldn't remember exactly when she picked up the

habit of drawing out the last word of any utterance: each syllable long, distinct, and deliberate, as if stretching out a roll of dough one more inch before cutting it into. He mused that girls nowadays liked to have a bit of Cantonese flavor in their speech.

"Sure," Piao said, just in time to swing the car sharply right onto Shanghai Road. He had to cut in front of a black BMW on the right lane to make the turn, and its driver, whose face he couldn't see behind the tinted windows, honked.

"Turtle's son!" he muttered angrily. "Just because he's driving one of those–"

"Sor-ry," Cuicui cooed in the back.

"Forget it."

She used to speak the Beijing dialect with a noticeable Anhui accent. He actually liked that better than this Cantonese-style drawl. Why? A whimsical preference, perhaps.

"How's the new home theater system?" Piao asked, as the car merged into the stream of traffic on the busy, tree-lined Shanghai Road.

"Fa-bu-lous!" Somehow, though, the old enthusiasm, a palpable excitement during a shopping trip, was not quite there. "I mean, it's like. . . sitting at the foot of a waterfall and hearing it all just crashing down. No static what-so-e-ver."

Yeah. He could imagine what it was like.

Recently, Piao had been toying with the idea of having an affair with Cuicui. He didn't really know when, how, and why it started. She was young, pretty, and lonely. Hadn't he read somewhere that such women were more prone to having affairs? As far as he knew, William came by only once or twice a week. How would she kill her time? Shopping took care of a chunk of that. Playing *majiang* with girls like herself helped a bit, too.

What else, then? She had left her folks in a small village hundreds of miles away and come to this coastal city several years ago, thirsting for excitement and a future for herself. Excitement she had found all right, but a future?

How would he start? What would be the first move?

He had taken her on shopping trips like this more than a dozen times now. Just the two of them, like a couple. Only that he was not the doting husband, or a remorseful lover. He was running an errand for William. That was all there was to it. William used to take her out himself, shopping or going to the movies. Nowadays he just played truant. Too many important business deals to take care of, he would say.

What would be the first move?

It had happened several times before. When she came out of one of those fancy plazas or shopping centers, and when he walked up to take over those flashy bags to put them in the car, their fingers would touch, their bare arms brush accidentally. Her fingers, her arms felt so soft, so supple, so cool, so unlike that of his wife, dry, unresponsive, no matter how much hand lotion or cream she had applied.

If he let that momentary touch linger just a bit longer, would that send her a signal? How would she respond? Would she get upset?

No. She turned to look at him instead, with a smile, an unmistakable tenderness in her eyes.

After parking the car outside her apartment building, he popped the trunk open and grabbed those bulging flashy bags. Their arms brushed once or twice again on their way up to her third-floor apartment.

He seemed quite at home here. Black and white tile floor, a frosted glass ceiling light in the living room, a cream leather couch against the wall on the immediate right, the new metallic-silver Sony digital home theater system nestling in the corner between the bedroom and the bathroom, a few silver-plated black and white photos of clouds, trees, creeks. . . .

In the dining room were a glass top black metal-framed dining set with four chairs, a small white fridge in the corner, on its top a 8x10 crystal-framed picture of her in a fresh red sweater, jewelry-free, fixing her gaze at the viewer, her back resting against a sprouting willow. Right next to the picture was a small vase of a lush asparagus fern.

Oh, yeah, there was the bedroom. Its door was ajar, through which he could see the corner of the pinkish puffy quilts on the mattress, the mirror inlaid in the creamy headboard.

"So, how's this new Sony set of yours?" he asked, amiably.

"Want to try it?" There was a nervous eagerness in her voice.

"Why not," he shrugged. "I'll have to warn you, though, I don't know a crap about new songs."

"I know," she winked coyly.

Unlike William, who had picked up quite a few new pop songs about pubescent or unrequited love, all he could howl were songs from the early days of the Cultural Revolution. He didn't see how groaning and moaning into the microphone would better his life one way or the other.

"How about 'What A Beautiful Jasmine Flow-er?'" she suggested, flipping through the DVDs in a box next to the machines.

"I know that one for sure," Piao said with zeal. "Picked it up back in Anhui, you know. But you'll have to lead me."

"No pro-blem."

She pressed the remote and placed a DVD in the tray of the machine.

A seventeenish village girl in a fresh red blouse, two long braids of rich hair resting on her curvy chest, a dreamy tenderness sparkling in her eyes, appeared on the 32" screen, strolled in the midst of teagreen jasmine shrubs full of budding flowers. . . toward him.

Cuicui, a natural, poured her heart into the mike. Her soft, silky voice floated up from the digital amplifier, caressing the very air he breathed, her eyes having the look of being transported to a faraway place.

Was this the look that William. . . .

Their voices were intermingled now, touching and brushing each other intimately, in perfect unison.

He felt his heart pounding urgently and tremors pulsing down his limbs.

Throwing the mike on the floor, he turned, grabbed her face in his hands, and proceeded to plant a thousand tender kisses on those cherry lips. She responded just as passionately.

He gathered her up in his arms. . . oh, she was so light, a basket of freshly picked tea leaves.

As he made the first step toward the bedroom, however, she suddenly felt so heavy. . . a rock the size of a car had fallen into his arms. . . he couldn't hold her anymore. . . he couldn't breathe. . . his lungs were about to explode. . . .

"Damn!" he grunted, slapping his right thigh.

The engine roared and lurched forward, like a cheetah breaking into a sprint after stalking a small antelope for some time.

"Are you all right?" Cuicui asked.

"Yeah."

He slowed the car down to a smooth stop near the curb. They were already outside the New Century Plaza. He could feel the 45-story bluish glassy presence towering over everything else in its vicinity.

Why would the fantasy screech to a halt, right there, every time, as if somebody had rammed a stick through a spinning wheel? Did it have anything to do with his chest now flat like a piece of onion pie? Well, the bulging muscles of his youthful days were gone with the wind—that was for sure.

"Should I come and get you after parking the car?" he asked when she pushed open the door and stepped out. A wave of heat whirled inside the car.

"No, I just want to check out a new digital cam-ra."

Before closing the door, however, Cuicui bent (he caught a glimpse of her creamy skin beneath the cut of her silky shirt and his breath quickened) and said, "Well, why don't you come and look for me on the third floor? I might want to look around a bit lat-er."

"Okay."

He turned into an alley and pulled into a parking lot behind the plaza. Toward the end of the lot, between a light gray Mercedes and a deep red Jaguar, he found a spot. His Santana 2000, though sparkling clean, looked like a crestfallen domestic rooster sandwiched by two proud peacocks with long shiny feathers. If only he were driving William's new Audi sports sedan.

What was the trick? How had he done it?

They were both in the seventh grade when the storm hit their school, well, the whole country, for that matter. Piao became a star almost instantaneously, a deputy commander-in-chief of the Red Sun Champions Corps, one of several such fiery Red Guard groups that had shot up on the campus of a small middle school in a less affluent part of the city.

He recruited William, who was known as Mingfang back then.

"Like to have some fun, too?" he asked Mingfang, who was huddling quietly in the back of the classroom which was in an uproar about how to have a denunciation rally against the principal ahead of every other revolutionary organization.

"Sure, but. . . what can I do?" Mingfang mumbled, timidly.

"Well, let me see," the deputy commander-in-chief said, his eyebrows knitting. "Aren't you good at brushwork?"

"Yeah."

"Well, I hereby appoint you Chief of Big Character Posters and Banners. How does that sound?"

"All right!" Mingfang almost jumped for joy.

From that moment on, Mingfang had been like a shadow following him just about everywhere.

Once he and millions of the other little devil champions nationwide had outlived their usefulness, they were sent packing to poverty-stricken rural areas of hinterland provinces to be reeducated by the peasants. He went to Anhui and Mingfang to Jiangxi and they lost contact with each other.

About ten years ago, at the first class reunion in a fancy Sichuan restaurant downtown, they met again. Mingfang, now known as William, had earned a master's degree from an American university and returned to represent a Fortune 500 company in China. He was the damned cocky star that evening.

"Like to work for us, Deputy Commander-in-Chief?" William asked before leaving, after an evening of feasting, reminiscing, and howling revolutionary hymns in the karaoke hall. He had a habit of mixing in an English word here and there in his speech.

"Sure, but what can I do?" Piao asked, blushing to his toes.

"Well, didn't you say you drive?"

"Yeah, I've been chauffeuring my general manager for a few years now."

Truth be told, he liked how the executive assistant title sounded, though his job description included executing all kinds of stupid errands besides being William's chauffeur. The pay was not bad, either: over three times more than he used to make at the heavy machinery plant.

Sometimes, when he saw William going over paperwork at his mahogany executive desk in his spacious office in the firm's suite on the tenth floor of World Trade Plaza; when he caught glimpses of his former follower, through the rearview mirror, listening to him chatting cheerfully with a pretty female associate or assistant, he would imagine their hands touching, their arms brushing, and would wonder: could he—Piao—the once proud Deputy Commander-in-Chief, have done the same?

He had fantasized about that, too.

He was in an American college classroom, a gray-haired, big-nosed professor was lecturing eloquently—in Chinese, of course.

He was driving a beat-up car delivering pizza to big mansions where people showered hundred-dollar bills on him for tips.

He was at the commencement, gown and sash and the whole regalia, tossing his cap up in the air, shouting "Hurray!" like the maddening crowd around him, when another gray-haired, big-nosed man, also in stupid regalia, had just announced something in a solemn voice.

He was at another class reunion, surrounded by the old buddies like the star he used to be, and even those girls who had been disdainful at the first reunion were now pestering him with all kinds of naïve questions. He was glowing, being nice to everybody, and having a swell time.

This fantasy of his would crash to the ground, too, because he was clueless how to get to the runway and take off. During the eight years in Anhui, he didn't study English at all. He read Dream of Red Mansions and a few of other banned classics, mostly out of curiosity and a desperate need to forget about where he was, but he had never thought that one day the gates of colleges and universities would be opened again. When they were in 1977, whatever he had got from those banned books was not enough to get him a ticket—each was hotly contested by about 20 or more eager, hungry people like himself—to attend. Without a college education in China, how could he dream of going to graduate school in America? He knew that in his fantasy he had conveniently started in midair and cruised to a smooth, joyful landing.

To be fair, William had treated him nicely. Because they went way back? Because William knew that he knew too much and that he could trust him?

Piao still remembered the first time he saw Cuicui with William at a karaoke hall.

William introduced her, winking at him proudly. "She's waitressing in a three-star hotel restaurant downtown."

She was like. . . like a jasmine flower budding on the slope of a hill of deep, dewy green: fresh, shy, and innocent.

"You've good eyes," Piao whispered, winking back.

Every time he saw her after that, Cuicui seemed to have shed a bit of that fresh, awkward naiveté. How? He couldn't put his finger on it. Perhaps with the addition of each new, fancier dress, each new piece of jewelry, and, ultimately, the gradual loss of her native Anhui accent.

William didn't hide anything from him. Well, he used to drive them to places anyway. Since William got himself a new Audi, things had changed. Lately, at least, William seemed to be breathing through the nose of the new assistant office manager he had hired several months ago, a 22-year-old college graduate, as fresh and pretty as the old Cuicui, and more vivacious. Her legs were long and slender, too.

Often when he walked past William's office, he could see his boss and the new assistant out of the corner of his eye, huddling behind a computer at the mahogany executive desk, their heads practically touching. He could even overhear William saying something in English, something funny, perhaps, and her resultant giggling in her soft, peachy voice.

Turtle's son.

At the end of the day, when he was leaving, they would still be in his office.

"Just tidying things up," they would say to him.

"Yeah, tidying your pants up!" Piao would snarl to himself.

When back at work the next morning, he would find himself staring at the burgundy leather couch right next to William's desk a bit longer than usual, and an odd feeling would well up in his stomach. Hell, there was nothing he could do about it.

"Mind your own business, pal," he mumbled aloud to

himself. "That's what you should do."

A fiftyish man, his arm around the waist of a pretty, twentyish woman, was coming out of the revolving door. He gave Piao a look and whispered something in the young woman's ear. She giggled. The uniformed usher inside the plaza greeted him with a wooden smile.

The first floor was cosmetics, jewelry, and arts and crafts. It was bright, glassy, shiny. In the air was a kind of supercilious elegance, vitality, and. . . coquettishness. The whole place seemed to be daring him to do something dashing so that his presence would not be completely uncalled for. And with each step, he couldn't help noticing those beautiful blondes in the flashy pictures displayed on the counters and just about everywhere. He could feel their warm, unbashful blue eyes touching him, their deep red lips, full, lustrous, maddening, pouting in his direction: "What are you waiting for?"

Would he dare? When the city was first invaded by a stampede of plastic blond models more than a decade ago, Piao was fascinated. Their tiny waists, curvaceous bodies, and bold eyes were so, well. . . refreshing. They stirred up something wild, something achingly delicious deep inside him. As he strolled throughout the store, gazing at their supple bosoms covered in tightly-fitting shirts or, worse, lingerie, he would feel his heart pounding urgently. During sleep at night, he would moan and toss and turn fitfully.

"What did you make all that noise for?" his wife would ask the next morning.

And lately Piao had caught his thoughts drifting back to the Cuicui-like girl back in Anhui, too. Oh, her childlike, innocent eyes, and the way she would glance at him in the fields, picking tealeaves, side by side.

"Do you like it here, big brother?" she would ask.

"Of course," he lied.

"Then, why do you still want to go back?"

His eyes popped with a big question mark.

"I just know."

She would blush. She would still come, roll up her sleeves and wash his clothes. She would bring him fresh spinach, tulips, chives, and other vegetables from her pop's garden.

There, in that Anhui village, from which it would take hours to walk to the nearest town to catch the once-every-other-day stop of a dusty, long-distance bus to get to anywhere, Piao was sort of a star, too. As the first and only middle-school educated young man in the history of the village, he would be asked by the mayor to read aloud any important documents from county, province, or central government for the benefit of the illiterate and semi-illiterate folks gathered on the threshing ground. He would often read and write letters for them, too.

She, on the other hand, was the prettiest thing in the village, prettier than almost all the girls in his middle school class.

Sometimes, on a moonlit evening, the two of them would sit by the little pond in front of his cottage, listening to the care-free chorus of frogs, eels, snakes, and crickets, breathing in faint fragrances of jasmine flowers floating in the air, feeling life itself quivering quietly across the fields and hills in the misty distance. There was no need to talk. There was not much to say anyway.

When it became very late, when she had gone home and he was back in the cottage and lying in his squeaky bed, he would want her badly, so badly, imagining what it would be like to hold her in his arms and kiss her dewy lips. Yet he wouldn't do anything rash the next day. He didn't want to be stuck in that "ghosts-wouldn't-lay-eggs" place forever. And he didn't want to mess up the girl and then just leave her behind, either.

The night before she was to be carried away in a bamboo sedan to her groom in a village on the other side of the hill, the girl gave him a freshly-knitted red sweater she had made for him. He cursed himself for days afterwards.

He still had that sweater in an old canvas trunk filled with little odd souvenirs, knickknacks, and whatnot.

Piao awoke from the reverie to see that he was already on the third floor.

There she was, still at the camera counter, chatting with a very nice looking salesgirl—damn, where had they found all these pretty chicks?—a new Nikon digital camera in hand.

"Old Piao," Cuicui turned to him and asked, "What do you think?"

She handed over the camera, their fingers touching, but he didn't dare let it linger. He looked into the LCD, pressed the zoom button a few times, and pretended to take a snapshot of her. She posed, smiling into the camera. That smile was for him, for him alone.

"Great!" he exclaimed. "How much?"

"Five thousand four hundred *yuan*."

"Not bad, not bad at all."

"Okay, Miss," Cuicui said to the salesgirl. "I'll take this one."

"Sir," the salesgirl turned to Piao, a smile on her face, "Cash or credit?"

"He. . ." Cuicui burst out laughing, "He's not my old man!"

He blushed to his toenails. Little bitch, couldn't tell? Did he look like a Hong Kong tycoon or something? He felt sort of flattered.

"Sorry, Old Piao." The laugh on Cuicui's face had melted away. "I didn't mean. . . ."

"It's okay," he shrugged gallantly.

"Here you go," Cuicui handed a Great Wall card to the salesgirl and turned to him again. "We'll let William worry about the bills, right?" After a pause, she added, lowering her voice, "one last time."

"Huh? Last?" he asked, lowering his voice, too.

"Yes." A more pensive mood seemed to be taking over.

"Didn't you say you wanted to look around after this?"

"Not interested any-more."

"What happened?" he asked when they were leaving.

"You should know."

Yeah, he had known it was coming, but not so soon.

Turtle's son.

They were quiet while taking the escalators downstairs.

"You wait here," he said as they got to the revolving door. "I'll go and get the car."

So William had decided to move on. Back to his wife and daughter in America?

Piao had seen them. William's wife, tall, freckled, short hair dyed to remedy the loss of luster and whatever was associated with it, a pair of thoughtful—no, moody—eyes, she had a PhD in biology or something, is doing research at a medical school. Their daughter—Emily?—was a lovely, robust, and intelligent girl. Which one of those top universities was she attending now?

Whenever they came to visit, about once a year, William

would be acting like a doting husband and indulgent father. He would take them to resorts and they would stay at the Hilton or Holiday Inn Crowne Plaza in town, as if their mansion-like residence in a gated compound in the most affluent section of the city was not good enough.

Unless. . . he had made arrangements with the cute assistant office manager? William had acquired a beer belly and lost quite a bit of hair on the top, but hadn't shown any signs of slowing down at all. Anyone speeding in the fast-lane of life like that was bound to break down or run into some fatal accident, sooner or later.

Piao couldn't afford to do all that himself. He had never taken his wife to the New Century Plaza and other fancy places. He knew that window shopping would only make him, and her, perhaps, feel worse.

They had been living in a small one-bedroom apartment for twenty some years. Last year he and his wife felt that their son had become too old to sleep in the small couch in the main room. So they cut their already small bedroom in two, separated by thin boards with frosted glass, with their bed, dresser, and nightstand cramped in the bigger half, their son's single spring bed and a chipped three-legged writing desk filling up the smaller half. That way, the son would have a place to study and prepare for college entrance exams. That way, he and his wife would not be able to make love any more. Well, truth be told, they hadn't been together like that since. . . when?

He had fantasized about buying a bigger apartment, three bedrooms, perhaps. With his wife being laid off from work, that dream had ground to a screeching halt. Poor woman, she might never have a chance to taste what luxury was like.

In this blue-collar apartment community, though, his family was doing all right. Everyday, when he returned from work and parked the Santana in the cement quad walled-in by old, gray buildings, he was conscious of eyes glancing in his direction.

"Old Piao, just back from work?" an elderly neighbor would holler at him warmly when he stepped out of the car.

"Yes, auntie," he replied, grinning happily.

Could he be Cuicui's old man? Sort of?

An interesting proposition to play with.

Cuicui would be throwing away money a thousand times faster than he could scrape up, one stupid errand at a time, to put in her palms. He—and his family—would have to slurp thin noodle soup every meal. But her. . . oh well, he'd have to leave that for later.

He and Cuicui remained quiet all the way to her home.

The uniformed guard sitting inside the gate room saw his car, pressed a button, and the gate slid open slowly.

Piao parked the Santana near an entrance of Building No. 12 in the back of the compound, popped the trunk open, and grabbed the flashy bags. She unlocked the metal security door with a key and he followed her up the stairway to her third-floor apartment.

Her long, lustrous hair rippled down her slender shoulders, her silky blouse hugging her shapely body intimately, her fleshy legs (who gave a damn about them being a centimeter or two too short) in translucent pantyhose moving titillatingly underneath her pinkish skirt. . . .

His breath quickened.

"C'mon in." Cuicui opened the door with another key.

There was a detectable tremor in her voice.

He stepped in and dropped the bags on the floor next to the leather couch in the living room.

The window air conditioning unit was humming somewhere. The light-colored curtains were drawn to block out the summer sun. It was cool and dim inside. She turned on a floor lamp in the corner. The living room basked in a soft, tender light.

"Old Piao, are you thir-sty?" she asked, the same detectable tremor in her voice.

"No. . . not really." He could hear his heart pounding a bit too loud.

She went to the dining room, opened the fridge, and got him a bottle of natural water anyway.

When she handed him the bottle, he felt her cool fingers linger in contact with his, just a bit longer than usual. Had he imagined it?

She picked up a remote on the coffee table, pressed it. Red, blue, yellow streaks blinked, glittered, and chased each other in circles on a panel in the new Sony set in the corner.

A veritable flood of a crystal clear, soothing melody filled the room. . .a seventeenish village girl in a fresh red blouse, two long braids of rich hair resting on her curvy chest, a dreamy tenderness sparkling in her eyes, appeared on the 32" screen, strolled in the midst of teagreen jasmine shrubs full of budding flowers. . . toward him.

Someone had floored the gas pedal in his heart.

Cuicui was walking toward him, a jasmine flower in full bloom. She got dangerously close, and stopped.

Would he? Would he dare?

His heart was racing like mad.

"Want to sing a few songs?" she asked, giving him a cordless mike, a palpable nervous expectancy in her warm gaze on him.

"I. . ." he stammered, "I've got to go." He cursed himself right away for having slammed the brakes on a fantasy that was roaring on the runway to take off into a dizzying sky.

What a beautiful jasmine flower, the girl on the screen began, sweet, as if in a dream.

Cuicui looked at him.

"I. . . I've got a few more errands to run." He could feel his heart throttling down angrily.

Fragrant, pure, blossoming in the early morning hour, the girl on the screen continued.

"Old Piao," Cuicui murmured, a whiff of that familiar, maddening fragrance already deep inside him, "will you come and see me a-gain?"

Vulnerable to slings of wind and rain . . . .

"Sure," he faltered, not daring to look Cuicui in the eye.

"Pro-mise?"

He nodded.

Shield you from malice and pain—as the soothing melody and the chorus in the background roared to a crescendo.

He reached out to shake hands. Her soft, supple hand, cool, almost cold, rested trustingly in his.

"Take. . . take good care of yourself," he struggled, let go of her hand, turned—caught a glimpse of her liquid eyes—and hurried out of the door.

The melody, the girl in fresh red, the clinging fragrance, the jasmine blossoms shivering on the slopes . . . were following his trembling footsteps.

"I'll be damned!" he mumbled.

As the car merged into traffic, Old Piao rolled down the windows to let the warm summer breeze blow full in his face, oblivious to the cityscape churning restlessly in the fierce rays of a flaming sun.

Big Mama

What was that?

He rubbed his eyes with his short, fleshy fingers.

It sounded like a little puppy being patted a bit too eagerly, but they didn't have a puppy at home The last thing he remembered he was rapid-firing his way through dungeons and blowing away enemy combatants into thin air by the hundreds. Well, he had been killed numerous times, too, but he could always bounce back with a new life and charge forward again.

The little clock radio on the nightstand said 1:07am.

The whimpering persisted.

As he rolled to the edge of the bed and managed to sit up, he could still feel in his belly the *jiaozi*—the stodgy, juicy, meat-filled dumplings—he had had for supper last night.

Wobbling to the bedroom next to his, he breathed heavily, his bare feet flopping against the tiles, which felt cold, hard, and ticklish.

The door was slightly ajar. A pale light from the full moon shone through the tall windows. He could make out the blurry shape huddling in bed.

"Ma, are you alright?" He asked, dully.

No reply.

"Ma?" He moved in and slouched down by the edge of the

bed.

"Mmmm." Ma sniffled. Her hair straggled across the pillow.

A mountain of tissues, wrinkled, balled, had piled up by Ma's pillow. Her long fingers reached into the box on her nightstand, but it was empty. He went to the bathroom, grabbed Ma's hand towel, came back, and placed it in her hand.

"Try to get some sleep, Ma. Tomorrow will be a big day."

Ma blew her nose into the towel and nodded.

"Go back and get some sleep, too, Feifei."

When Feifei flopped backward on his bed again, its frame cringed in response to his weight. Perhaps he needed a bigger, sturdier bed. Would he bring that up tomorrow?

The fog in his head had cleared a bit. His sleepy eyes wandered from flashy posters of Yao Ming and the Nameless from "Hero" to the framed picture on the wall opposite his bed.

Pa, though not really handsome and his hair beginning to thin on the top, was in good spirits. Ma smiled happily. A high school girl kind of smile. Like one of the girls he sometimes saw on his way to school. Most girls, even those from his own class, would giggle loudly among themselves when they saw him tramping along with a bulging school bag balanced on his fat butt. But that girl—oh, she had such long, vivid eyelashes—would nod and flash him a faint smile.

And in that picture he was a happy two-year-old nestling snugly between Pa and Ma. He looked a bit chubby, but there was nothing in his rosy-cheeked face that promised that in a few years he would blossom into a ridiculous miniature Japanese judoka with everything, his head, his hands, his belly, his bottom, and his fat thighs, twice the girth of kids his own age.

Everything had been picture perfect. Until his seventh

birthday. Pa took him and Ma to the fancy restaurant at the top of that grand Shangri-La Plaza downtown on that cool, cloudless October evening. Their table was by a huge window from where he would feel the cityscape, well-lit against a steely-dark sky, churning out there. When he had made his wish—"You want the moon in the sky and I'll go and get it for you!" were in the beaming eyes of both Pa and Ma—blown the candles, and cut a big slice for everybody, Pa stood up and went to the restroom. The cell phone Pa had left on the table buzzed. Feifei grabbed it though Ma frowned.

"Shiwei, is that you?" He heard a woman shrieking.

"Shiwei? Who is Shiwei?" he blurted, confused. "You want to talk to my pa? Pa's name—"

"Who are *you*?" The woman sounded as if she had just fallen splashing into a barrel of Sichuan chili sauce. "Hah! You must be that heartless turtle's son's son!"

"Who is it?" Ma looked alarmed.

"Some mad woman wanting to talk to a Shiwei." He covered the little gadget with his fat fingers and whispered. "Must be a wrong number."

"I told you not to play with Pa's cell phone! Give it to me!" Ma looked more frightened than when a crow cawed in the leafy canopy right above where they were setting up a picnic not too long ago. The ugly bird, startled by a pebble Feifei threw into the thick foliage, cawed again evilly, took off, and fled.

Pa was already back. He scowled, tearing the phone from Feifei's hand, and walked away. When he at last put the phone to his ear and started talking, Pa sounded so apologetic, like when he was caught running the red light on their way back from the picnic.

"Who is it, Ma?" Feifei became worried, too.

"I don't know." Ma mumbled, her eyes frozen in Pa's direction. "Your Big Mama, perhaps."

Big Mama? He had never heard of Big Mama.

"Yeah, you should call her Big Mama." Ma turned her gaze back to her son, a forced, reassuring smile on her face.

Big Mama called again—more than once—after that birthday dinner. He knew, even though he never dared to touch Pa's cell phone again. A few days later, Pa left for another business trip. Only this time he didn't return until several months later when it began to snow. He looked so deflated, so tired. The old gaiety in his eyes was gone. And they didn't go to the Shangri-La Plaza or any other fancy place to celebrate the reunion.

"What happened to Pa?" He asked Ma, whispering, the next morning at the breakfast table. Pa was still in bed.

"Pa had a bad business trip. That's all. Don't you worry." Ma smiled. Her eyes looked swollen, though, as if she had cried.

Then Pa went on his longest business trip, ever. He didn't come back for his son's eighth birthday. Ma, alone, took Feifei to the same restaurant to celebrate.

"Want to tell me the wish you made?" Ma asked when he was digging into the fat slice of cake on his plate. Feifei didn't reply. He knew that Ma knew what he was wishing for.

It was around this time that he began to dream of hearing quiet whimpering in the middle of the night.

"Did you cry last night, Ma?" He wanted to ask at the breakfast table the next morning, but didn't have the nerve. Poor Ma. What would happen to her, and him, if Pa— he didn't dare to finish the thought.

And Ma began to dote on him even more. Whenever he

didn't feel like eating at home, Ma would take him to a KFC or McDonald's in town. She would just sit there and watch her son biting into mouth-watering chicken drumsticks and sandwiches as if he hadn't eaten for days. One time, Ma overheard two girls at a table next to them giggling about Feifei being a little fat, gluttonous pig. She whirled around and gave the girls such a withering stare that their faces turned frosty white instantly.

Pa did call around his birthday and big holidays. But every time, Pa sounded like he was in a big hurry, like he was watching his back, like he was a fugitive from one of those DVD movies they had bought from the street vendors. Every time Pa told him the same story: he was on an important business trip and the first chance he had, he would come back and see him and Ma.

That first chance presented itself yesterday evening when Feifei was smashing into the enemy ranks while Ma fed him *jiaozi*. He was too busy fighting decisive battles to come to the dining table. The phone rang. Ma was going to answer it, but he rose from the floor and grabbed the phone first. He didn't remember ever getting up from his fat butt so fast before.

"Hello?" He gasped into the phone.

"Feifei? Is that Feifei?" It was Pa! Pa still sounded like a fugitive being hunted down.

"Where *are* you, Pa? Ma and I have been—" He turned to look at Ma. The bowl in Ma's hand shook like a bomb had just landed inside their apartment.

"How've you been, son? How's your—"

Pa stopped abruptly, as if someone had jabbed him in the back with a gun. Feifei heard a door being slammed in the background and a woman—she sounded faintly familiar—saying something sharp. Pa found his voice again, but was speaking as if he were a complete stranger.

"Tell her to meet me at 11:30 tomorrow morning."

"You want to talk to—" Feifei asked, but Pa had already hung up.

Ma had so many questions for him afterward that he didn't know which one to answer first. And he didn't have answers to any one of them, anyway. Yet he had a pretty good sense who that woman in the background was.

She and Pa? She and Pa and Ma, and Feifei?

Feifei turned in bed. A full moon today. A good sign for tomorrow?

He yawned and drowsed.

"Feifei, get up." A familiar voice sang by his bedside. The sun is already shining on your cute, little butt!

"Still early, Ma." He mumbled. He wanted to drift back to sleep again.

"It's already 7:30! Remember today's a big day?"

He slowly forced open his eyes.

Ma had already washed and done her makeup. She had put on her best clothes, too. Ma was still young, and pretty, but the high-school girl-like look in her face was long gone. Her eyes looked swollen despite the careful makeup.

By the time he finished breakfast—two large meat-filled steamed buns, a boiled egg, and a glass of milk—it was only 8:30, still too early to leave. He and Ma sat on the sofa, watching the second hand in the clock on the wall making its rounds. When it became too boring just sitting on his butt, waiting, Feifei turned on the TV, plugged in his video game console, and fought a few more battles, but only half-heartedly. Ma, he noticed while his fleshy thumbs tap-danced on the controller, stood up and went into the bathroom he didn't know how many times.

When they finally stepped out of the taxi and hurried up the steps to the entrance of the Shangri-La Plaza, Ma instructed once again. Be polite. Don't behave like an ill-bred brat and make Ma—and Pa—look bad.

It was only 11:00 in the morning, but the restaurant was already filled with diners. The food on the buffet counters looked and smelled as rich, bountiful, and mouthwatering as he remembered. He felt a pang of hunger as his stomach growled.

Then he saw Pa, sitting at a table near the huge window. Upon seeing him and Ma, Pa straightened up in his seat, as if a megavolt current had jolted his body, but dropped back in his chair right away. He looked smaller, and the hair on his head—all grayed now—was much thinner.

The first time his classmates saw Pa at one of those teacher-parent conferences, they made fun of Feifei afterward: "Is that your *grandpa*?"

A youthful-looking grandpa, to be sure, an embarrassed and angry Feifei had retorted in his mind. He couldn't say that about Pa now.

Feifei felt another pair of eyes on him, and Ma, too. It was from an elderly woman sitting opposite Pa. She was tiny and skinny. The tight silky dress she had on didn't help much in shielding the bony frame of hers.

Have you just returned from Somalia, Rwanda, or something was on the tip of Feifei's tongue, but he remembered Ma's instruction.

Pa coughed to clear his throat.

"I don't think there's any need for me to introduce—"

Ma nudged Feifei forward, smiling, but he could feel Ma's hand trembling.

"Call 'Big Mama.'" Ma urged.

So this is Big Mama! Feifei stood as if in a trance and let his eyes wander in the empty space between Big Mama and Pa. He felt something rushing to his head.

"So, *this* is the little whore!" Big Mama sneered, looking at Ma, and at him up and down, critically. "And this is the little turtle's son!"

"Lower your voice," Pa begged. "No need to make a scene here."

Big Mama's bony hands on the table were shaking nervously.

"So," she said at last, "You're the whore who has stolen Shiwei from me?" She lowered here voice, but her words were hot as chili sauce and sour as vinegar.

"You know how Shiwei and I started twenty-five years ago? We were dirt poor then. We had just returned, as sent-down youths, from a ghost-wouldn't-lay eggs place in Jiangxi—"

All the dots in Feifei's mind had been connected now. A mix of shame and anger brewed inside him, but he didn't know exactly why.

"I'm from Jiangxi," Big Mama murmured in a voice as if she had become bodiless, "And I bet you a thousand *yuan* that you were not born yet when we were there." She gave Ma another sneering look.

"Ai!" Pa sighed. "It's no use talking about those days again. Let's eat first."

"You've clean forgotten those days, Shiwei!" Big Mama raised her voice again. "That's why your heart has rotten through, your conscience. . . ."

Feifei stole a glance at Ma, Pa, and Big Mama, stood up, and navigated through eager diners to the buffet counters. A man had to eat even if the sky were collapsing down on his head.

When he made his way back, with a mountain of steak, meatballs, and prawns piled up in his plate, Big Mama, Ma, and Pa were still where he had left them.

Big Mama, looking up in the middle of a sentence, grunted through her nose:

"No wonder your son is such a big, fat, ugly piglet, Shiwei! Doesn't he look like the pig we raised back in Jiangxi? We were so hungry. Our meat ration was less than one or two *jin* a month. But that pig would grow fat on just about anything, grass, old vegetable leaves, whatever you could find to put in its trough. When we slaughtered it on New Year's Eve? Oh my, the big, fat feast we had—for days! Remember those days, Shiwei?"

"C'mon," Pa begged, standing up. "Let's go get food."

Ma started to stand up. She appeared to rise, slowly, as if floating.

"Food! Food!" Big Mama continued to fume, getting to her feet, too. "All you can think of is food. How can you produce anything better than that between you two?" With that, Big Mama tilted her head toward Feifei with a look of disgust.

Why don't you pee and take a look at yourself, you ugly, foul-mouthed witch! That was what snapped into Feifei's mind as he sat down to eat. Oh, the steaks tasted so delicious, the meatballs so juicy. Pretty soon his fingers were sticky with sauce and his face smeared with sauce, too. He used the napkin to try and clean himself, but only succeeded in turning his face into a bad map of the world.

Ma came back to the table with a few pieces of Nanjing

fragrant duck—he should get that, too, for the second trip—and green beans on her plate, followed by Big Mama, whose plate had only a few paper-thin slices of smoked fish to show for it. Ma walked with her head low on her chest, like a school girl being reprimanded by a stern teacher.

"Why don't you leave him alone, you shameless whore!" Big Mama was still babbling as she sat down. "You should have seen how hard we lived during those days! We didn't have a penny. We had to be on our knees to borrow from seven aunts and eight uncles and just about any grandpa and grandma we knew! I had to stand by the door and holler to get customers. Don't you stare at this old, bony package of mine. In my day I was quite a looker!"

Pa returned to the table. He frowned and sat down.

"Then," Big Mama continued, "Our store became too small for Shiwei! He wanted to seek bigger fortunes elsewhere. That was when his heart was eaten by dogs, his conscience torn to rags by giggling whores like you from nowhere!"

Why didn't Pa say anything to shut Big Mama up, to protect Ma from her vicious words? But Pa seemed so busy with his food.

"What sin have I committed to have all this misfortune dumped on me?" Big Mama's voice suddenly dropped to a low murmur filled with pain and confusion. "First my little boy. . . ."

Ma lowered her head, trembling visibly.

Ma—Feifei begged in his mind—don't you fall for the crocodile tears from that old witch!

"Shiwei played truant, leaving me alone, all by myself, in a big house for months and months!" She snickered at Pa and turned her face back to Ma. "No, he doesn't deserve you! Let him go. Look at me! Take a good look at me! How much time do I have on this earth? When I am gone, I don't give a damn what kind of disgusting sin you two will cook up between yourselves!"

Ma buried her face in her hands. Pa was looking out the big window.

No, I can't take this any more, Feifei decided, and stood up. He had to go for more food. He had just started and had barely filled up a corner of his stomach.

Navigating his way around and between the buffet counters, he helped himself to one more steak, one more meatball—how could he resist?—several pieces of meaty Nanjing fragrant duck, a few slices of smoked fish and green beans—Ma said he needed to eat more vegetables—and topped it off with a large piece of cake complete with creamy frosting.

When he tramped back to their table, Feifei noticed a little commotion there. Big Mama was on her feet, shaking her index finger in the face of a terrified Ma, so vehemently, so threateningly close, as if—

I felt a voice from somewhere deep inside crying: "No. . . No. . .No!"

Feifei charged forward with the plate in hand. He felt something inside him boiling up to the roots of his hair.

He saw how Ma, Big Mama, and Pa all turning to look at him, shocked expressions on their faces.

You miserable, vicious, ugly witch! He cussed in his mind. I'll blow you up into thin air!

Nearing the target, he raised the full plate above his head like a stone.

"No. . . No. . . No!"

He heard a familiar voice screaming. He felt the stone being knocked out of his hand and a blinding light which stung his cheeks. He tripped and fell flat on his face on the shiny, glassy tiles. A second later the plate clanged and clattered next to him.

"You ill-bred brat!" It was Ma screaming, scowling down at him. Her face had never looked so twisted, so old, so ugly. "She's your Big Mama! Have you swallowed leopard's bile? Pick up your big, fat ass and apologize to Big Mama, now!"

He cringed back on the floor when Ma reached out to pull him up.

What had happened to Ma? She'd never hit him even once all these years, not even when he deliberately forgot homework assignments, not even that time when he skipped school and went to play video games at the loud arcade near home.

Big Mama appeared by Ma's side. So did Pa.

"C'mon, sis, don't be too hard on him." Feifei heard Big Mama scolding Ma. "He's just a little kid."

Bewildered, Feifei sat there, frozen.

Big Mama bent closer and gave him her hand. He could see the bluish veins underneath her thin, pale skin.

"Let's go and wash your face," she murmured in a voice completely drained of the chili sauce and vinegar. "Just you and Big Mama, how about that?"

Ma nodded, her eyes misting. Pa sighed.

Feifei brushed off the meatballs and whatever food that had landed on him, and reached out to grasp Big Mama's proffered hand. It felt so bony and small in his own.

The Long March, Sort of

Recovering from the mouthful of exhaust being farted out of the tail of the big beast, he cursed the turtle's son, his entire family, and his bottomless ancestors eight generations back, with all the obscenities he could recall and rehash at the moment.

Then he started to crawl again.

Ah Sheng used to love the smell when he was still a small dim-witted kid in an emperor's whip-couldn't-reach and ghosts-wouldn't-lay-eggs village by the Yellow River that would burst the dyke and bury the mud-and-thatch huts in tumbling waters during the flood season and dry up to the last drop and crack up big time in dead winter.

One sweat-dripping summer afternoon, a beetle buzzed somewhere in the sun-baked distance. It kicked up a cloud of dust along the narrow mud road as it trekked nearer. The buzz rose, stirring up the pressure inside his young bladder to an urgent need for immediate relief, until the pristine country air trembled in a strange, dizzying odor.

The beetle—no, the beast, for it felt like a big, presumptuous beast—came to a halt, doors opened, and hearts thumped as shiny leather-shoes landed on the ground, causing the mud powder on its surface to arise in a billowing cloud.

The crowds at the rural elementary school—a single mud-and-thatch affair with wind-kissed windows—leapt into frenzied clapping and chanting.

The human wall was too high, too thick for the kid to push through and catch a glimpse of the beetle and its proud cargo. The big toes kept sneaking out of his torn, Mama-made cloth shoes as his bony elbows navigated in the thick of uncles, aunts, and grannies just as eager to feast their eyes on this once-in-a-lifetime apparition.

Minutes later, the beetle was heard buzzing again. It kicked up a cloud of dust on the narrow country road. Its buzz fell until it could be felt only as an absence. But that strange, dizzying odor lingered in the air for hours, for days, and imprinted a vague but ineffaceable consciousness in the mind of the young boy that there was another way of life; a much bigger, more exciting world loomed out there, somewhere, beyond the limits of his small, poor, out-of-the-way village.

Now, more than twenty years later, as he was crawling on a cedar-padded country road far away from home, Ah Sheng hated the smell. He cursed and spat and cursed some more until the beast tucked its tail, sucked in its fart, and vanished into a speck in the distance.

And he hated the turtle's son of a driver. The man had no business dumping that kind of insult on his head:

"Don't you motherfuckers want to live any more? Looking for death?"

Even though his vision was somewhat blurred by the bone-cracking wind, he could see the disgust in the driver's face against the glare of the late afternoon sun. He had tried to stop the car in the middle of the country road. It screeched to a halt. The turtle's son rolled down the window, screamed, and turned to someone in the passenger seat—a pretty young woman—and said something funny, perhaps, and they both roared with a hearty laugh. His good arm and good leg were not fast enough to maneuver and position his body strategically when the vehicle swerved to one side of the road and puttered away.

By now Ah Sheng had become quite skillful in coordinating his body movement with the fingers and elbow of his left arm and the toes and knee of his right leg. The right arm and left leg were not good any more. Misshapen with bones sticking out at wrong places, they were as good as dead. They had become useless, cumbersome appendages that had to be dragged along as the fingers of his left arm gripped the hard surface of the ground, the weight of his upper body being propped up by the elbow, while the toes and knee of his right leg gave a teeth-clenching forward kick.

In the beginning, when he could still hear crickets chirping in the quiet of a starry night while dozing off in the bushes by the roadside, the right arm and left leg, freshly broken, were a bit more annoying than being useless burdens. It used to take mountains of motherfucking obscenities to appease his prickly nerves as he slithered and wriggled along, a few inches at a time, on the sun-scorched hard ground during the day.

He hadn't wanted to hitchhike. He knew that with his shoulder-length wild hair, his smoke-smeared face, and the rags that revealed more than shielded his emaciated body, nobody in his right mind would give him a ride. He looked an exact copy of that proverbial twiggy, weedy grasshopper in his elementary school textbook, that lazy, happy-go-lucky insect who had dawdled away his spring and summer and autumn days singing carefree songs and then had to drag his ass to the door of the ant's well-heated home on snow-hushed evenings and beg for a morsel of food.

All he had wanted from the driver was to know whether he was going in the right direction. He could not afford to get lost again. Truth be told, he didn't know exactly where his home county was. Closing his eyes tight he could only recall a blurry outline of the yellowed map of China on the wall of that single mud house school and he knew, vaguely, that his home county was hundreds of kilometers to the southwest of the place where he had worked for a bit over six months before his misfortune happened.

Ah Sheng had been slithering and wriggling through villages and towns from string-thin footpaths between wheat fields to cedar-padded country roads to broad and smooth and shiny expressways that stretched monstrously toward the skyline, flooded with noisy big-headed, bright-eyed beetles and beasts of all sizes and shapes and colors.

He had been depending on the kindness and expected the not-so-kindness of strangers for food, water, clothing, and occasionally, shelter.

"You want food? Here's your food!" A young man had held a steamy bowl high in the air, tilted it, and laughed shrilly, a crowd of curious spectators looking on, as hot, soupy noodles poured down into the open palm of his good hand, his emaciated, dog-tired body huddling in the middle of a busy street.

"No, ma'am, don't be fooled by his pitiable appearance," a middle-aged man ladling out lunches from behind a cart stand around a busy street corner said to a woman tourist. "I've seen them all. He could be a millionaire for all we—" The man stopped when the woman bought a box of snow-white rice topped with stir-fried vegetables and a big, juicy steak and carried it over to him.

One time he had dozed off in the chill of a late autumn night under the eaves of a small, old mud house in a small village. In a fitful dream, his home village was being buried once again in the roaring waters of the Yellow River and he caught glimpses of his sickly wife and seven-year-old daughter holding on to something atop the roof of their home.

"Ah Sheng, come and save us!" His wife's desperate shriek pieced the maddening night.

"Papa!" He could see the fright in his darling daughter's rain-soaked eyes.

He jumped into the thundering waters.

No, he shouldn't have left his home. Flood-plagued, ghosts-wouldn't-lay-eggs kind of place, it truly was, where folks still ate and breathed and farted pretty much like their ancestors centuries before them. Yet what did it matter if he could be with his wife and daughter again? He had seen with his own eyes another way of life: multi-laned expressways, skyscraping high-rises, modern shopping centers and residential compounds; he had even touched the burning hot steely body of his boss's brand new car! So the young and restless from his village who had come back—for short visits—and painted a picture of prosperity and opportunities of the outside world were not really exaggerating. But what did all that have to do with him now? Nothing. Zero. Not a fart. Worth no more than a picture of a freshly baked green onion meat pie that he could only feast his eyes on but couldn't sink his teeth into.

Yet he had left his home. He had been tempted. He had wanted a tiny slice from that pie, not by begging, of course, but through hard, honest work, and Heaven knew that he was willing to do hard work and do just about anything so that his daughter could go to school—at least a few years of elementary school—and start a life elsewhere, anywhere but the place where the soil had dried up long time ago, having been plowed and sowed and forced to yield for Heaven knew how many centuries, and not another drop of juice could be squeezed out of it no matter how hard you fussed and messed with it.

These thoughts—he marveled that he could have lucid thoughts even during a fitful dream—hit him as he kicked and struck forward in the surging waters, toward what was formally his home. Somehow he was still full-limbed and his arms and legs were as stubborn as the mind of a lean, quick-tempered man. He had taken in a mouthful of muddy water from a wave, spit it out, struggled to breathe, and continued to strike ahead through the thunderous night.

The water began to thicken. A deep mass of tiny, brown ice formed all around him. He couldn't move any more. He was frozen in solid ice, like a human specimen in a glass jar of a museum.

Suddenly, the sun burst through. The ice began to melt away. The last breath of warmth in his heart spread to the rest of his body.

Ah Sheng shivered and woke up from the dream.

He was being covered with a cotton-padded coat with an oily, tobacco-stained collar. An old auntie was standing by his side, gazing down at him with pain in her eyes.

"Sin! What sin!" Auntie murmured, shaking her head.

He struggled to sit up. The ground was still wet. The browned grass and bushes all around still dripped with chilled raindrops.

Auntie had in hand a bowl of congee with pickled turnip and a roll of corn pancake wrapped around a couple of green onions. She watched, sighing, as he attacked the food like a ravenous dog. When he thanked Auntie for her Buddha-like heart and got ready to resume his journey, she stuffed a few more rolls of pancakes in the pocket of the dark-gray coat.

"Keep the coat. My old man's, you know. Wherever he is now, he has no use for it any longer."

By now, about two months later, the old coat had become a thin, sorry shadow of its former self. It had holes around the left elbow and elsewhere and the tobacco smell around the collar was long gone. Would it last him through the winter? How was Auntie now? He could still picture her thin figure and worry-lined face as she stood in the early morning chill watching him slither and wriggle away.

Ah Sheng had lost count of the days he had been thus traveling. All he knew was that it was still summer when he was being shown to the door of the county hospital. He didn't know how he had gotten there and how long he had stayed. Someone must have found him by the roadside that horrible night. He had not died. The doctor and nurses attended to his broken arm and leg the best they could, he figured, and told him to leave. Since he couldn't pay for staying in the hospital for further treatment, there was nothing more they could do for him.

Ah Sheng continued to crawl along the country road against tear-drawing wind.

Bicycles, tractors, and occasionally dust-covered buses, minivans, and cars dinned and hummed and sputtered by. Except for a curious, contemptuous glance at the figure creeping along the edge of the road like an awkward insect, nobody bothered to stop. They were all in a hurry to get home or wherever their destination happened to be. He didn't try to stop them for help, either. He didn't want to risk that turtle's son of a driver kind of wrath again.

The sky had thickened with a gloomy mist. It looked like it would snow tonight. It was about time. As the old saying went, good snowfall in winter meant good harvest the following year. He didn't know how much wisdom there was in that saying because he had seen many a good, heavy snowfall in winter that failed to harbinger a good harvest. Still, by sheer nature of someone who had been tilling the same soil his ancestors had generations and generations back, Ah Sheng decided that when he got home, he would buy the best wheat seeds he had heard folks talking about, which could yield at least 600 kilograms of grains per *mu*; he would deep plow his farmland—all 25 *mu* of it—one more time to get it ready for sowing in spring. How would he manage the plow and the cow, single-handed and single-legged as he was now? He didn't know. Nevertheless, he figured that if he could harvest 15,000 kilo of grain and sell a big portion of it at the market at 20 cents per kilo, he couldn't become rich, but would probably be able to put aside a small sum for his daughter's education.

A faint smile appeared around his cracked lips. He had gone through the same calculations numerous times while wriggling along between sky and earth, long before the thought of snow had entered his mind.

He could handle snow, Ah Sheng figured. Thick, deep snow. He could dig a hole with the bare fingers of his good hand, crawl in, curl up, and have a nice sleep inside. What if he could not wake up the next morning, what with the cold and the empty stomach and all? He could picture his body stiffened like an icicle buried in white snow. It wouldn't be too bad a way to end it all, he sighed. Yet something deep inside him still wanted to wake up—when the sun rose—and drag himself out of the hole and get on his journey again.

The dusk deepened. The world between sky and earth blurred. The air was thickening with night, wavering under its own weight. A Sheng hadn't seen a single house along the stretch of the country road he had covered in the last few hours. He hadn't had a morsel of food since morning. His fingers and toes trembled weakly as he made each new effort to move his body a few inches forward.

He stopped again to gasp for air.

His heart leapt with hope when his searching eyes spotted the vague outline of something a bit further off the road to the right, a structure of some sort standing alone in the flat fields embalmed by the deepening mist. He turned and slithered along a narrow, stubbly path in its direction with renewed vigor.

It was a small, low shed: a thatched roof supported by four willow poles. Perhaps the owner of the fields around had set it up as a kind of sentry post to guard whatever he was growing—potatoes, tomatoes, melons, corn, wheat—during the harvest season.

He saw a shadow stirring inside the shed. The shadow had seen him, too.

"What the hell? What are you?" It was an old man's voice.

The accent was more akin to that of his home county than those he had encountered before. "Are you man or ghost?"

"Man, big Uncle," Ah Sheng mumbled weakly. He must look more disgusting than that twiggy, weedy grasshopper. Surely more frightening in the gathering dusk.

The frosty-haired old man had a long-handled spade in his hands. He stepped closer, bent to take a better look at Ah Sheng, and shook his head.

"Sin!" the old man murmured. "What sin!" His tremulous breath had a familiar tobacco smell to it. "What happened?"

"I—" Ah Sheng choked.

"Forget it. No need to tell me," the old man sighed again. "I've seen worse."

A pause.

"I live on the other side of the hill," the old man said. "Just about to call it quits and go home. See, with the first snow coming, I thought it'd be a good idea to till the soil one more time to get it ready for spring."

Ah Sheng nodded vaguely. He would love to chat with the old man about growing potatoes, tomatoes, melons, and wheat, but he was blindingly weak.

"Muddy Waters County, how far is it from here?" He gathered enough strength to ask.

"Muddy Waters? Not far. Not far at all. One day's walk, if you—" the old man stopped, eyeing him sheepishly.

When Ah Sheng mentioned the name of his village, the old man responded warmly, "Oh, yeah. I've heard of it. Bachelorsville. What a sad name. One of our village's daughters-in-law is from there. Juhua. She says no girls there would—"

Ah Sheng felt an exploding urgency in his bladder even

though it was more than half empty at the moment. This was the first time ever someone had given him a definite answer that he was not too far away from home.

The old man fumbled in his pocket. “Look, I still have a steamed bun left. My old woman, you know. She was worried that I’d be starved. But what does a man as old as me need that much food for?” He chuckled.

Ah Sheng took over the bun with trembling fingers, brought it close to his nose, and sniffed nervously. Then he took a bite, and chewed slowly, rolling it in his mouth left and right and up and down to savor it.

“Young folks nowadays,” the old man murmured and straightened up. “They don’t want to till the soil no more. But you can you grow corn cakes and steamed bun on asphalt roads and shiny expressways, for Heaven’s sake?”

The old man stepped outside the shed, looked up into the sky, and turned to Ah Sheng: “Looks like a big snow.”

He chuckled again and walked into the misty night. A few snowflakes drifted down, rested on his frosty head, and vanished instantly.

More snowflakes, big, goose-feather sized snowflakes, began to fall, vivid, muffling, turning the world all around the shed into a fairy-tale kind of show, a show that was put on for him, Ah Sheng, alone. No. For the old uncle, too, who was trudging through the night to go home.

Ah Sheng placed the bun between his chin and his left shoulder blade, held it there, and reached out his hand. A few snowflakes floated down and settled on his palm. They felt cool. Gently he rubbed them against his dry lips. Then he took another bite from the bun.

As he was chewing, Ah Sheng suddenly felt the presence of something, somebody else nearby, not very far off. He was not alone. What could that be? A vagrant like himself? A homeless ghost?

He searched with his eyes in the snow-hushed night around the shed.

He looked into a pair of unblinking green eyes, three or four meters away from where he was. He could feel the warmth from its nervous, hurried breathing as it watched him, its tongue hanging from its mouth.

It was a dog. A stray dog, perhaps, its black and white coat already wet with snow, revealing the skeletal outlines of its skull, rib cage, legs, and haunches.

It noticed that he had noticed its presence. Its face twitched. A few timid, baby-like whiny noises escaped its mouth.

Ah Sheng made a threatening gesture with his good arm. Startled, the dog turned to run, but checked itself when it saw nothing more sinister following the threat. It stood its ground, its eyes fixed on him, on the bun in his hand.

Ah Sheng took another bite from the bun, waved his good arm at the dog again, and grunted loudly through his nose to add seriousness to the threat. The dog turned to run again, but stopped when it didn't see any lethal projectile thrown after it.

The poor thing must be very, very hungry, too, Ah Sheng thought. He stopped chewing. Half of the bun in his hand was already gone, but he could still hear hunger rumbling against the walls of his stomach. Even if he gulped down the whole of whatever was left of the bun, that wouldn't be enough to fill a tiny corner of his stomach.

He looked up and looked into the eyes of the dog again.

They were fixed on him, on the diminished bun in his hand, patiently.

He took another bite from the bun and spat it toward the dog with such sudden forcefulness that the dog jumped, spasm-like, but regained its composure almost instantly. It approached cautiously, sniffed, licked up the piece of bun with its drooling pink tongue, and chewed excitedly.

What was he going to do? He needed the food to last him till tomorrow morning. A man's life was more precious than that of a dog. That was for sure. He took another big bite from the bun. It tasted good. He would need ten more such sweet buns before his hunger was satiated. Yet a dog's life? It was a life, too, even though it wasn't much of a life.

He turned to look at the dog again. Its pink tongue was still licking the lips of its bony mouth, its eyes fixed on him.

What the hell, Ah Sheng thought and threw the remainder of the bun to the dog.

The dog lurched, licked it up, and devoured it between ravenous groans.

The snowfall had thickened. The world was being laced with a layer of pure white. Except for the groans from the dog, all was quiet. So quiet. Slowly, cautiously, Ah Sheng fell back on the hard earthen ground and stretched out his good arm and good leg. Would he freeze to death sleeping like this in the open? Not in the open exactly. He had a thatched roof over his head, all right, but snowflakes could still drift in and fall on his face. What if he wouldn't wake up tomorrow morning? He shivered at the thought and shrank further into the wind-soaked coat. He needed something warm. Something that would prevent his body from being frozen into a stupid icicle. Something like a stove with live, red-hot coals. Something as hot as the kilns where he had worked for over six months.

The Good Fortune Construction Material, Inc. was right outside Sea Breath, a satellite town of the provincial capital. Before one of the young and restless from his village had talked him into leaving home and traveling hundreds of kilometers to this place of opportunity and prosperity, Ah Sheng had never seen a bricks or shingles kiln.

A bricks kiln looked like a huge castle, the size of a grain threshing ground, oval in shape, its walls going up at least seven or eight meters high, its tall chimney puffing out fiery smoke into the blue-black sky. It had a dozen or so entrances for loading green bricks inside its hollow, arched stomach and unloading bricks when they were fired.

The first time he stepped inside to unload, not long after they had turned off the fire, Ah Sheng was hit by a wave of dusty, white heat that almost snuffed him out. He felt his skin parching and heard the juice inside his body evaporating thunderously. Panicking, he stepped out to gasp for air.

"C'mon, brother," Young Zhao, who had got him the job and was training him, turned and shouted to be heard over the huge electric fan placed at the mouth of the entrance. "Don't ever let the boss catch you chickening out like this!"

Even with the thick canvas gloves on, Ah Sheng could feel the fired bricks burning into his fingers as he grabbed four or five them at a time to load onto a big two-wheeled barrow. When the barrow was filled with fired bricks, he would pull it through a narrow, steep road and unload the bricks in an area for trucks and tractors to transport them to construction sites of high-rises and residential compounds. Some of those fancy buildings he had seen would stagger and tumble down, probably, if he were to pull out from their walls all the bricks that had his fingerprints burnt into them. He was willing to bet a month's pay on that.

For ten to twelve hours a day, six days a week doing that kind of backbreaking labor, Ah Sheng was paid seven hundred *yuan* a month. He figured that was only a fraction of how much his labor was worth, but to whom could he complain? And compared to tilling the soil that had long dried up, at least he was making money.

Besides his little daughter's education, Ah Sheng figured, he should try to put aside some money so that one day he could start a small business of his own. What kind of business could he run and how much it would take to get it started? He was rather vague there.

All of his dreams, though, were crushed one hot afternoon when, going downhill on that long, steep path, he couldn't hold steady the barrow and had a head-on collision with a car coming from the opposite direction. To avoid being crushed into a meat pie between the metallic beast and the barrow, Ah Sheng jumped in the air and landed on the hood of the car. As he fell, his hands reached out, instinctively, to support his body. That was the first time his fingers had ever touched the burning hot steely body of a goddamn car.

The driver stepped out of the car, grabbed the collar of his shirt wet with sweat, dragged him off the hood, and hit him hard in the face, big diamond rings sparkling in the sunshine.

"You motherfucker! You know what you just did? You

messed up my car! My brand new Lexus!"

Ah Sheng knew he was in trouble. The man, sunglassed, potbellied, turned out to be none other than the boss, the sole owner of Good Fortune Construction, Inc.

The boss turned to check the car. His thick fingers felt the scratches on the brilliant gray hood where the shafts had hit and the bricks had tumbled.

"I'll pay for the repair," Ah Sheng offered in a trembling voice.

"You pay for the repair? You lousy, worthless motherfucker!" the boss whirled around, his mouth foaming with fury. He grabbed Ah Sheng's collar again, threw him on the hot, pebble-surfaced ground, and sat astride his back. "You know how much it'll cost? Your whole goddamn life is not worth my car!"

Ah Sheng tasted blood oozing inside his mouth. He turned his head to breathe.

"This is how you pay for my car!" He felt the boss's diamond-studded fists pounding away on the back of his head.

A sudden pause.

The boss was trying to grab something.

Something heavy and sharp-edged landed on his arms and legs.

Ah Sheng fainted before he had time to scream.

When he came to again, Ah Sheng found himself lying somewhere in the thick of wild weeds on a hill; crickets, grasshoppers, and nameless other insects were crooning happily. Above was a boundless dark blue night sky filled with twinkling stars.

He didn't want to die there. He wanted to move but couldn't. That was when he found his right arm and left leg had been crushed.

Between crawling with his good arm and good leg, rolling, and fainting several times over, he managed to get to the bottom of the hill where he saw a cedar-padded country road. He blacked out again and when he awoke, he was in the hospital.

The snow had stopped. The world around the shed had turned a freezing white. Ah Sheng shivered and curled up into a small ball. Something else stirred near his feet. He raised his head to see. It was the dog. Its head was resting between its forepaws, its sleepy eyes half closed. As if to acknowledge its company, the dog opened its eyes wider, blinked, and rested its head between its paws again.

Ah Sheng fell back on the cold earthen ground and began to drowse. Yes, he needed to catch some sleep so that he would have enough strength to resume his long march. He was not too far away from home now. Once home, he would buy the new wheat seeds and deep plow.

The Girl in Blue Jeans

She was a nervous wreck the first time she went to that hotel near Drum Tower Square and wandered outside its grand entrance. She didn't know why she was there and what she was doing. Okay, she knew why she was there and what she was doing but she didn't *really* know.

It was that time of an early spring day. The sun had just set and the city lingered in a hazy blur before tumbling into the chilly darkness of night. Without even looking up, she could feel the hotel's tall, slick structure thrusting forty-five stories into the dusking sky. Some of its numerous windows, like so many scales on the body of a gigantic fish, were already glowing with faint, yellowish light. She had never been inside a hotel like that. The world on the other side of the shiny brass revolving doors seemed to be whispering in a subdued, jazzy kind of mystery. Men and women—oftentimes older men and younger women—were being sucked in and spat out as uniformed concierges hurried to help with luggage or guide them to the long line of waiting taxis.

Zhaodi paced nervously up and down the marble steps of the hotel's entrance. Her heart thumped like the footsteps of the beast she would encounter in a weird dream a few months later. Several other young girls, all wrapped in tight clothing to show off their curves, were hovering around the entrance like flies, too. Perhaps I should leave, she thought to herself. This is no place for me. She turned and descended the marble steps again.

"Hey, you!" a man hollered from behind. "The girl in blue jeans!"

She stopped. No other girls hovering there had on blue jeans. Her jeans were sky-blue, the kind of blue where you could soar like a lark. Yet, caught in the pale glow of the golden, violet lights from the entrance, her jeans looked purple, hideously purple.

She glanced back without turning. The silhouette of a man was standing at the top of the steps. Behind him were the brass and glassy doors.

"Yes, you," the man quacked in a much lower voice now that he had her attention. "Want to come in with me?"

As if obeying a command she turned and climbed back to the top of the steps.

The man looked her up and down, grinned, and grasped her cold, quivering hand.

"First time? College girl?" He asked in a more confidential kind of tone. "I like college girls."

Zhaodi didn't remember much of what happened after she entered the hotel, the heels of her sneakers almost hit by the overeager revolving doors. Everything was a blur and she was like one drifting through a dream and watching things happening to someone else, some other girl in blue jeans: how she was frightened by the muffled sound of a mini-waterfall thundering down an artificial stone wall from the second floor; how she paused when passing by a grand piano with a mirror-like ebony finish, amazed by its black and white keys dancing up and down, left and right, all by themselves, as if being played by a pair of ghostly hands; how the coconut juice the man ordered for the girl tasted so white, sticky, and sickeningly sweet; and how the people beside and all around her murmured, giggled, and laughed with such strained gaiety, some soft music—saxophone? clarinet? cello? she had no clue—swirling in the background, like some long, sneaky fingers massaging somewhere deep inside her.

She couldn't remember much about the man, either. He was not young, or handsome, for sure. His hair, well, what did she care about his hair! One thing about him, though, she did remember. His smell. The mixed odor of a tobacco addict and a victim of chronic indigestion that he forced into her mouth right after he shut the door of the room on the 39th floor.

It seemed like a lifetime later when she had dragged herself back to her dorm, she brushed her teeth left and right and up and down and inside out until they bled and rinsed a thousand times, but even today, she can still smell him in her mouth.

And she did remember what the man said in his stinky voice, as if disappointed, when he had peeled off all of her clothes:

"Oh, you're so goddamned skinny!"

As the man fussed with her skinny chest and legs and hurt her badly, Zhaodi was lying on the big bed, as if dead, but all the time acutely conscious of the girl in blue jeans she had left down there, outside the hotel entrance. She seemed so small, like an ant, and was gazing up at the window of the man's room on the 39th floor.

"Ma," Zhaodi murmured as she and Ma wandered from counter to counter and store to store in the town of their county. "How many times do I have to tell you? I don't need much. Just a pair of jeans, maybe. Really."

Zhaodi and Ma were on a shopping trip to help get her ready for college. She had just received the official admission letter from CCU a few days before. They had been like ants on hot stove ever since the college entrance exams were over early July. By the time the letter reached them, it already looked so wrinkled, having passed through so many hands, because they are rural folks and don't have their own mailbox. Ma, who has only two years of elementary school, went through the letter over and again between her trembling fingers. Even Pa, semi-blind thanks to a weird illness, with no more schooling than Ma, wanted to take a look at the letter himself, just to make sure it was not a practical joke. Her eight-year-old brother was "Sis" this and "Sis" that the whole time as if she had answers to all the questions in the world.

That evening Ma went to the chicken coop so that she could cook something nice for her daughter and for the whole family, but she couldn't decide which of her hens to slaughter. Reed Flower had been so dependable, an egg a day for over a month now; but so was Daisy; Blackie hadn't done well lately, but she had been busy hatching. Each of them squawked and clawed so heart-wrenchingly in Ma's hand that she had to let them all go.

"Forget it, Ma," Zhaodi said. "We can celebrate just the same."

So they celebrated with an extra dish of scrambled eggs mixed with chopped cucumber and a small cup of some cheap rice wine for Pa.

Pa had been sick most of the time. Their small mud-and-thatch cottage was always filled with the bitter aroma of some weird herbs simmering in an earthenware pot on the stove. Pa sometimes helped with the family's 18-*mu* farm, but it was Ma who carried everything on her shoulders: cooking, washing, seeding, weeding, and harvesting. When she was still in middle school, Zhaodi liked to go to the fields to help hoe the weeds or fertilize the wheat every now and then, but Ma and Pa didn't want her to stay long.

"Go back to your books," Ma would say, dabbing her forehead with a small towel on her shoulder. "You don't want to grow up and marry the yellow earth, like Pa and me, do you?"

Pa would lose his temper and shout some obscenities if Zhaodi lingered just a bit longer even during harvest time. As she walked home, she would glance back and see Ma, back bent so low, cutting into the sea of golden wheat with her sickle and Pa feeling his way around to tighten up the felled wheat into neat bundles.

Zhaodi's parents had an unfaltering, almost mystic belief that their daughter would amount to something one day when she grew up. They began to believe so, she was told, the day she survived a drowning accident. She was about three years old when it happened.

She was wobbling around and babbling whatever nonsense to keep herself entertained while Ma and Pa were busy in the fields, not very far from where she was. She didn't remember what really happened. Perhaps she was chasing a butterfly or something. She wandered just out of sight and fell, headlong, into a deep pit filled with human and animal waste and dead leaves and murky rain water. She didn't know how long she struggled in the pit, or whether she swallowed anything while kicking and clawing down there, but she did remember how it felt the moment her desperate fingers caught the edge of the pit.

When Ma and Pa heard her crying and came running, she was already out and standing by the pit. She was caked, from head to toe, with murky slime, and rubbing her eyes with sticky fingers. She can still recall the rotten fish kind of stench in her nose. They knew that it had to be a miracle that she was still alive. They were sure—though she didn't have the faintest recollection—that a white-haired old man must have given her a helping hand despite the fact that she was nothing but a cheap girl.

From that day on Ma and Pa tightened their belts harder and worked longer hours in the fields so that their daughter could really amount to something. In the mountainous region where she was from, not many girls could afford to go to school. The Magnet Middle School she attended served six or seven villages, but she could count the girls in her homeroom class on just one hand. With Pa being sick often and Ma having to take care of the fields and the pigs and the hens all by herself, Zhaodi's family could barely scrape up enough to pay for her school. Every evening, while lying in bed, drowsing, she'd hear Ma and Pa going over, in hushed tones in their room, what little money they'd already saved, what money they would expect to make with the eggs, wheat, melons. . . .

Naturally, anything she did at school, every lesson, every assignment, she would give it more than her utmost best. She didn't want her parents to be disappointed.

Physically, though, she was a late bloomer. With the kind of food she was having every day, she doubted she'd ever bloom at all. She was a vegetarian on a strict diet involuntarily. The first time she saw a patch of red in her underpants she was already 14 years old. And for a long time her chest was so flat she began to doubt if she'd ever develop real breasts. She was not tall, either, but she had long legs. Later, when some of her college friends who are bothered by their waist lines asked what her "secret" was, she could barely contain herself with a laugh: You want to be slim? Try to live like me for three days and you'd be better than slim!

The evening she received the college admission letter; they sat at the small, crippled dining table going over, for the tenth time, the list of expenses for her first year in college:

Tuition:	5,000 yuan
Fees:	1,200 yuan
Books:	500 yuan
Room:	1,000 yuan
Meals:	1,400 yuan
Transportation:	500 yuan
Miscellaneous Expenses:	500 yuan

The total came to. . . 9,600 *yuan*!

Pa sighed deeply, taking a plaintive drag from the butt of his long-dead cigarette. Ma sighed and went about adding the figures up one more time to see if it would come down a bit. Zhaodi sighed and stared at the naked 40-watt light bulb hanging above the table. Her little brother? Oh, he was already dozing off on the little bed in the room he and she were sharing. It had been a long day of excitement for him, too.

Ma said she had managed to put aside 1,257 *yuan* in a savings account. Selling the two almost-fattened pigs could bring in about 400 *yuan*, if she could bargain for a good price. The eight sacks of wheat grain in the small barn behind the cottage, about 1,000 *jin* altogether, could bring in another 250 *yuan*. She had collected another basket of eggs, about 10 *jin*, and right now eggs were about 8 *yuan* per *jin*. . . .

They listed every penny they could find and just about anything that could be sold and came up with a total of about 2,500 *yuan*.

That left them 7,100 *yuan* short.

Then they listed every aunt, uncle, granny, or distant relative of theirs that they could think of from whom Pa and Ma thought they could borrow a few hundred *yuan* on account of some real or imagined favor they'd done them years and years back.

Zhaodi had never thought that earning top grades and getting accepted by a good university was actually the easiest part of the whole thing.

That was why she told Ma during that shopping trip—it was a trip because they had to walk for two hours to get to town—that she didn't need to buy much new clothing for college. She could use most of her old shirts and shoes. She'd be happy if she could get a pair of jeans, which would probably last her through the four years of college and beyond. Nothing fancy or expensive. No fancy Levi's brand. That would cost several hundred *yuan* a pair. But the color had to be right, neither dark blue nor the bleached kind as if the color had been washed off completely. It had to be the kind of blue that would look warm during the winter months and wouldn't look too warm early summer or autumn. So she settled for sky-blue. Sky-blue was natural, dreamy, not too assertive yet carried a palpable amount of confidence. That was how she felt about sky-blue.

What she didn't tell Ma that day was that she'd wanted a

pair of blue jeans for a long, long time. They were doing this grammar drill in the subjunctive mood in an English class during her ninth-grade year. It was a dialogue. The teacher asked her to be this cowgirl in a picture, and a boy she liked, secretly, of course, to be a cowboy. Both the American cowgirl and cowboy looked so cool in their blue jeans and large, felt hats. She knew then that she would look good in blue jeans, too.

Somehow, though, when she finally stepped into a pair of blue jeans—sky-blue, the least expensive kind she could find—and pulled them up, she felt so empty; they felt so fat and loose on her. Her wheat-straw legs and monkey-thin butt couldn't fill up the jeans.

"Don't worry," Ma said, her voice quivering, as she tugged at the waist and the bottom to make the jeans fit better, "you still have a couple of years to bloom."

She didn't get up and go to classes the morning after her first time at that fancy Drum Tower hotel. She'd never missed class before. She wasn't really sick or anything even though she had a mild headache. She just didn't feel good.

"Are you okay?" Juhua, one of her roommates, asked, feeling Zhaodi's forehead with her cool fingertips.

From the moment Juhua appeared in the dorm last September dragging behind her two striped plastic bags of clothing and books, Zhaodi knew she and Juhua would be friends. Juhua was a country bumpkin, too. Zhaodi could see it in her clothes, in her eyes, and hear it in her voice. They get along with the other two girls, Vivian and Elizabeth, just fine, but these two were different. They came in their parents' expensive-looking cars. They brought so much stuff with them as if they had moved into the dorm permanently and filled up every inch of space they could grab. And from the look in their eyes Zhaodi knew they didn't think much of her and Juhua.

No, she'd never envied Vivian and Elizabeth and the kind of things they have, CD Walkman, digital camera, laptop, and the other stuff. She didn't really need them to do well in college. But the 7,100 *yuan* that she and her family had borrowed was constantly on her mind.

For a long time she was having no more than half a vegetable dish for lunch or supper. One time a middle-aged server behind the counter gave her a large, juicy meatball on top of the half cabbage dish she had ordered. As she was leaving, she overhead him whispering to a coworker:

"See that girl in blue jeans? She could be blown away by a gust of wind!"

Zhaodi had never gone to his counter again.

And, of course, she had to wash her clothes every night 'cause everything she had, socks, underpants, shirts, she had no more than three pair. Sometimes, if it didn't stop raining for just two days, the clothes would be only half dry when she put them on. Needless to say, Vivian and Elizabeth weren't thrilled when their freedom of movement was hindered by her washing hanging from a long string across the small room. She didn't blame them. She would probably be annoyed, too, if her parents had arranged for a woman to come and collect her dirty clothes and straighten out her bed and things once a week. She just didn't know what it feels like to live like that, though.

She wore her jeans almost every day.

"How come you wear the same blue jeans every time you come to my home?" a girl she was tutoring commented one day, scooting her little butt further away from Zhaodi.

"They are my lucky charm, you know," Zhaodi said, matter-of-factly. "That's how I got accepted by CCU."

The girl was impressed.

Zhaodi and Juhua started to offer tutoring service to school kids about a month into their first semester. Even though she was way over her head with school work, Zhaodi was tutoring two evenings and Saturday mornings and was making about 100 *yuan* a week. Imagine the first time she held in her hand the money she had earned with her own labor! Zhaodi began to pay for her own food and put aside about 50 *yuan* a week. She figured that at this rate she'd need 142 weeks—almost three years—to pay back the 7,100 *yuan* debt. And she'd be accruing new debt in the meantime.

When she got up one Saturday morning toward the end of the semester she noticed that Juhua's bed was empty. She was alarmed. What was going on? When she returned from the tutoring session close to noon, Juhua was in bed. She still had her makeup on, yawned profusely, and didn't want to talk. Zhaodi got really upset.

"Tell me what's going on, young lady!" she demanded, grabbing a corner of Juhua's quilt. "Or I'll throw you on the floor! I mean it!"

Juhua obliged a few short, reluctant sentences.

Seeing the shock in her eyes, Juhua cooed, sleepily:

"No big deal. Really. Look around. Who isn't doing it anyway?!"

"Vivian and Elizabeth," Zhaodi protested, feebly, "and most of the girls I know."

"Vivian and Elizabeth?" Juhua grunted, "How many of us have their kind of parents? Besides, I didn't see them in the dorm either when I came back."

Zhaodi had no clue where Vivian and Elizabeth had spent the night and many other Saturday nights, either.

"Besides," Juhua said, turning on the side, yawning. "Who could argue with a few hundred *yuan* a night."

Zhaodi did a quick math: earning money at that speed, she would be able to retire the debt in 16 or 17 weeks, within one semester!

She blushed with anger at herself for having done such a calculation at all. Yet she caught herself going over the same math every now and then for the rest of the semester and throughout the time she spent at home during the Spring Festival.

Shortly after she returned to school for the new semester, she received a letter from her little brother, sent without her parents' knowledge, that Pa was seriously ill again. That was all that was needed to push her over the edge.

"Foolish girl!" Juhua, or Jen, as she now preferred to be called, burst out mirthfully once she figured out what Zhaodi was mumbling through chattering teeth. She was sitting by the edge of Zhaodi's bed, her eyes glistening with laughter. "Who told you to go about it *that way*? You've got the right to choose, too!"

That was how she started to go with Juhua to these places, bars, fancy hotels, and so on. She even adopted Connie as her English name though she hadn't used it often. Most of the time she just sat in the booth pretending to be listening to a man bragging about himself and the places he had been to while trying to fend off his greedy hands and legs underneath the table. Only occasionally when she ran into someone she sort of liked, she would go with him to his place. The first month alone she made more than 2,000 *yuan*! When Ma and Pa received the 2,500 *yuan* she sent them, they cried. Ma said, in the letter she wrote in her excited, uneven handwriting, that Heaven has eyes to have sent them such a daughter. But Ma cautioned that she should be wary of the traps big cities were known to be filled with.

And, strangely, Zhaodi started to bloom when she was almost 19. Her chest became fuller and her butt rounder and could actually fill up the blue jeans. She didn't look as pale, either. Even in places like bars and fancy restaurants where pretty girls are one *yuan* a dozen, she'd be conscious of men's eyes wandering on her body. No one, not another man, insulted her with "You're so goddamn skinny" ever again.

She also bought a few new things, a leather jacket and some cosmetics, nothing fancy. She needed them. Her ambition was to pay back all the debt and, if possible, save a bit for her little brother, too.

The night before she knew something was wrong, she had a weird dream.

She was alone on a long chain bridge between two jagged cliffs on a cold, dark evening. She was about halfway over when she suddenly felt the planks underneath her feet quake nervously. She looked and saw a huge beast thumping toward her from the other side! She wheeled around to go back because she didn't want to be crushed to death by the beast charging toward her. But all the planks behind her were gone! There was nothing left but bare chains and thickening dusk all around her.

Just then, she heard a voice from below:

"Jump, Girl in Blue Jeans! Jump and you'll be safe!"

The echoes bounced eerily between the cliffs.

Holding tight to the icy chains, she peeked below and all she saw was a dark bottomless unknown.

The chain bridge quaked more menacingly. She could smell the beast's sickening hot breath now.

The voice from below called again:

"Jump, Girl in Blue Jeans! Jump and you'll be safe!"

It was taunting, alluring, and terrifying, all at once.

She closed her eyes and jumped.

She was crashing to her death, a clean and instant death. She could hear her life whistling away from her body at the speed of light. Then it'd all be over.

Suddenly she felt herself being caught by something, like a blanket, yet she couldn't really feel a thing because whatever it was that caught her was both shapeless and invisible. She was floating in midair, arms open, as if she were airborne with an enormous parachute.

The sky was cloudless, sparkling with warm sunlight. Beneath her were butterflies, an ocean of them, green, yellow, pink, spotted, rainbow, the whole color spectrum; they were buzzing, waltzing, and forming and re-forming to the melody of her favorite tune: "Blue Danube." It was an amazing sight! Further below she could make out a small waterfall cascading down a cliff, windmills, endless fields of lush green baby wheat and nauseatingly sweet, mellow yellow rape flowers. . . .

She would have liked to be drifting like that forever but the next instant the butterflies vanished. Not a shadow of a single one left. The sun had fallen out of the sky, too. The world became a dark, bone-chilling cold blur again. And once again she was crashing down and her life was whistling out of her at the speed of light. She screamed, and screamed, and woke up to dizzying safety in her dorm bed.

She had the same dream a number of times, with some variations. Sometimes she was jumping off from a cliff, sometimes from the window of a tall, fancy hotel, but always at the invitation of that alluring voice:

"Jump, Girl in Blue Jeans! Jump and you'll be safe!"

That morning in mid-May when she woke up from the weird dream, she had a pounding headache and a bad fever. Juhua went with her to the university infirmary. The doctor there couldn't find out what was wrong with her so he sent her on to a municipal hospital. There, they ran a whole series of tests on her, blood, urine, X-ray, even CT. It was the longest and the darkest week in her life waiting for the results in the hospital bed. She feared the worst.

When the reports finally came, she felt like being struck by Five Thunders from Heaven. Why me? Why me? Why not those other girls? Why not those goddamn turtle's sons? Why didn't they want to have that stupid rubber thing on? Why? 'Cause they didn't like it that way! 'Cause it wouldn't feel good! Those turtle's sons can go to hell!

When the doctor went on to explain how he was going to use the latest treatment—some kind of cocktail therapy—to fight the virus, Zhaodi didn't hear a word at all. As soon as the doctor and his entourage of interns left, she struggled out of bed and staggered out of the hospital.

"Where?" the taxi driver asked without looking back when

Zhaodi lumped down in the backseat.

"Don't know, and don't care," she mumbled weakly. "Anywhere there're no people, perhaps."

A couple of hours later, she told the cabbie to stop and got out.

She was on a stretch of highway miles outside the city walls. On both sides of the highway were farm fields with lush green young wheat that stretched endlessly.

She waded into the sea of green until she couldn't walk any more and until the highway had dwindled into a faint, barely audible buzz.

She lay down, stretched out her limbs, and gazed at the sky above her. For a long, long time her mind was a complete blank. Did she doze off? Did she die? Did she melt into the dreamy kind of blue way, way up there, vanish into its soothing, seductive folds?

When she came to again, her joints had stiffened from the chill of the luscious, absorbent green blanket underneath her. She sat up and got on her feet again. As she trudged back to the highway, the sun had already fallen off of the horizon, but a small portion of the sky was still holding on to the last streak of bloody red before succumbing to darkness.

Nowadays the jeans look loose, even fat, on her again. She hasn't looked at herself in the mirror for weeks, but she knows she's probably no more than a shadow of her skinny self when she started college about a year ago. There are days she feels so low that she'd hear that voice again:

"Jump, Girl in Blue Jeans! . . . ."

Would there be butterflies to catch her if she jumps? Would

the white-haired old man give her a helping hand again? She doesn't know. So she refuses to listen to the voice. The worst so far is nausea. The world would just swirl and swirl until everything inside her has whistled away.

There're days, however, she doesn't feel anything at all, like today.

Vivian and Elizabeth moved out when they knew she was in trouble. She probably would have done the same too. In the beginning when she dragged herself back to class, nobody wanted to sit near her. The seats in the lecture hall would be left empty several rows deep all around her as if she were a plague or something. Things have gotten somewhat better lately, though. Even Vivian and Elizabeth came back to see her once.

Juhua is an angel. She couldn't have pulled through so much without Juhua.

Her parents? Oh, they don't know. How can she tell them? And her little brother?

Fatherhood

As he and Jordan squeezed into the reed mat-covered backseat of the small taxi, Anming couldn't help being amazed again by how much the kid had shot up in the last couple of years. Elbows resting on his knees, eyes fixed on the Adidas bag sitting on his big feet, Jordan hunched forward awkwardly, as if he didn't know what to do with his long arms and legs. There was that familiar look in his eyes, though, that nervous excitement in his audible breathing every time something big was coming up. And something big, really big was coming up: his team's very first All-District Middle School Basketball Championship game.

"You'll miss the opening ceremony, Anming," Miaomiao, his wife, turned her head from the front passenger seat and said. Her voice quivered with excitement, too.

"I don't want to miss it, either." Anming could hear the nervousness in his own voice. "And I've got to make it to the office to be sure everything is adjusted properly, or the test results would contain errors and all our work for the last several—"

"You could have asked Tiezhu, or—"

"Ma, it's okay," Jordan glanced at his watch and mumbled. "The game won't start until ten. Almost two whole hours away."

"The last thing I want," declared Anming as he leaned forward and laid his hands on the top of Miaomiao's seat. He was conscious of his fingers touching her long, silky hair tied together loosely with a fluffy, glittering purple ribbon and felt a sudden, familiar stir in his belly. "The last thing I want is to ask a friend to cover for me when I am perfectly capable of doing the job myself!"

He winced at what he had just said. A slip of the tongue, perhaps, but. . . did Miaomiao catch the undertone, the extra sound that had bounced off from the plucked string?

"Okay," Miaomiao sighed and then she said in a more playful tone, "Don't worry about it, though. I'm in control. See?" She turned again and patted the black, genuine leather camcorder bag sitting on her lap. "After all, I'm the third best photographer in the family. Trust me."

Trust her? In this day and age, could anyone trust anyone else in the whole world?

"Of course. I can't wait to see your masterpiece," he tried to sound playful, too, leaned back, and turned his eyes to Jordan.

"Who's the best photographer, then, Ma?" Jordan looked up and asked. "Me or Pa?"

"Yeah, me or Jordan?" Anming pressed, as if he really cared.

"Let me see," Miaomiao pretended to be deliberating. "Mmmm, the last time I checked, we had several minutes of blackout in the tape and the basketball court bounced around like a crazy dancer or a headless grasshopper. So, the gold medal has to go to. . . ."

What else could he expect from his wife?

"See?" Jordan turned and flashed him a toothy smile.

"Two gang up against one. What else is new in this family?"

He rolled his eyes exaggeratedly and threw his arms in the air.

"C'mon! Be a good sport!" Miaomiao giggled mirthfully.

Suddenly they all became quiet.

He turned his eyes away from Jordan and looked outside the window blankly.

Anming still remembered that evening 15 years ago. He had been waiting inside and outside the delivery room at the Number One Municipal Hospital since two in the morning. He didn't want to miss the first cry of his son—they had known it would be a son thanks to an ultrasound test three months before. His and Miaomiao's parents took turns waiting with him and bringing in breakfast, lunch, and supper in thermos containers. When, close to midnight, amidst gut-wrenching moaning and screaming, the doctor emerged from between his wife's legs with a bundle of pink flesh and announced: "Look, there's your little rice wine pot between the legs!" Anming was ready to drop to the floor and roll, tearfully, with joy.

Perhaps he was by nature a worrying sort of man. None of his buddies seemed to have fretted as much when their wives were due. Then again none of them was an only son. He had lost his elder brother—a mere toddler then—to a stray bullet during a shootout between two warring Red Guard camps during the Cultural Revolution. Besides, none of their wives was as pretty as Miaomiao and he wanted to make her the proud mother of a son, too.

Even today Anming didn't know for sure what the prettiest girl in the whole of the Yangtze Chemosynthetic Products, Inc. could see in him. His three years of Night College would pale miserably in comparison to whatever degrees those young engineers proudly displayed on the walls of their offices. Several of them had shown interest in Miaomiao in less than subtle ways. One continued to press his case, with blushful notes, movie tickets, and small gifts, even after it became public that Miaomiao and Anming were engaged. Neither was Anming nearly as tall and handsome as, say Tiezhu, and a few others among his buddies. Back then, how many girls at the company would have jumped at the first opportunity to take a ride behind Tiezhu on his grand, sparkling Honda motorcycle, the envy of all the young men in the company? Miaomiao did ride with Tiezhu a couple of times—just to satisfy her curiosity, as she explained later.

He had asked Miaomiao on their wedding night when all the guests and his loud buddies—oh, they were so full of mischief that evening—were gone, just to be sure. She pointed her pinkish index finger at the tip of his nose, pouted, as if annoyed by the question, and cooed: "I'm yours now, every ounce and centimeter of me. Isn't that proof enough?"

Then, for a long while, Anming was gnawed by the worry that he might not be blessed with a son. Not that he had any doubts about his own virility. Not that he wouldn't like to have a daughter who, he had no doubt, would turn out just as pretty as her mother. Yet since they could have only one child, the choice had already been made for them. On and off the basketball court and at *majiang* tables, his buddies used to tease him endlessly and rival each other gleefully with surefire folksy tips. Tiezhu, the loudest and cockiest among them all, though, had a baby girl born to him three months before Anming became a father, too.

The day after the ultrasound test, Anming felt like the weight of a mountain had been lifted from his shoulders. He was all over the company's basketball court during the two-hour lunch break, dribbling, passing, stealing, and jump shooting with such confident velocity as if he were ready to play Michael Jordan one on one. He even succeeded in blocking Tiezhu—the usual star on the court and almost a full head taller than Anming—several times by grabbing a rebound and jumping to dunk the ball into the basket. Miaomiao and the dozen or so spectators cheered loudly while Tiezhu, crestfallen, shook his head in disbelief.

That evening was when he and Miaomiao decided to name their son Jordan. Back in 1988, Michael Jordan was not a household name in China. Anming had caught a few glimpses of the NBA superstar on CCTV's sports programs and was dazzled by the way the man could literally fly in the air to dunk the ball into the hoop.

The cab stopped right across from the entrance of Jordan's school. The visiting team from the other school in their red and blue jerseys, and their fans, were getting off several long buses. A few crowds of students and their parents were gathered inside and outside the entrance and engaged in animated conversations. More people were arriving in twos and threes. Someone was testing the microphone in the school's sports stadium. Anming felt a knot tightening inside him.

Jordan sat up straight, grabbed his bag, his left hand on the door handle, like a young cheetah crouched and ready to leap.

"Don't worry about winning or losing when you are on the court," Anming instructed. "Just focus on the game and you'll be fine."

Jordan turned to give him a nervous, toothy grin, his chest

heaving visibly, but didn't say anything.

Jordan stood in the middle of the street now, waiting for his mother to join him. Then the two of them walked together across the street toward the school's entrance.

"Watch the traffic!" Anming rolled down the window and hollered.

The kid had certainly shot up so much in the last couple of years, he wondered again as the cab pulled into the traffic. A full head taller than his mother.

Anming had loved basketball since the elementary school. He was fast, agile, and had a very good spring in his legs. However, after a growth spurt between 13 and 16 he stopped growing at 167 cm. No matter how long he hung from the single bar, from the door frame, from a tree branch, from just about anything high that he could grab and hold on to, Anming could not add one more mark in the penciled chart on the wall in his crammed bedroom. Soon he became the shortest on the school basketball team. Everyone else went on growing. Tiezhu didn't taper off until he had reached 185 cm.

Although he had since made peace with his height and learnt to live with whatever he had got, Anming vowed that he would do whatever was in his power—except his genes, perhaps—to see that his own son would not suffer from the same mishap of a giant being trapped inside a dwarf's body. Giving his son an auspicious name was a good start. He took care to follow it up with all the surefire tips from the desk *Encyclopedia of Family Medicine* he had bought right after Miaomiao became pregnant, and from the several parenting magazines to which he subscribed. A sizable portion of their monthly pay went to purchasing the newest baby nutrition products: strengthened milk powder, calcium supplements, 100% natural juices, all of which promised to enhance a child's physical development. Every five or six months he and Miaomiao would take Jordan to the hospital or a mobile health information stand in the park to have their son's growth assessed.

"172 cm," doctors would announce warmly after weighing Jordan and measuring his length and factoring in the vital statistics of his parents. "Your son has a good shot at that height, to say the least."

Anming would have been more thrilled if the projected height was 175 cm or 180 cm, but he was a down-to-earth kind of guy and was happy that at least his son had a chance to break beyond the live-or-die 170 cm mark.

By the time Jordan was ten, he was already at 135 cm, in lockstep with most of his peers. The boy loved basketball, too, and was very aware of the advantages of being taller on the court. How many times had Anming seen his son measuring himself by the life-size Michael Jordan poster with a growth chart? The poster, a gift from Miaomiao's brother who had taken a business trip to America, almost reached the ceiling of Jordan's room.

"Pa, you want to see how tall you are, too?" Jordan urged him when they first nailed the poster on the wall in Jordan's room.

"No. I don't want to hurt Michael Jordan's feelings," Anming joked but blushed self-consciously, like every time he had to shake hands with a much taller player from the other team on the court.

"C'mon!" Miaomiao teased. "As if I don't know how much you've got between your head and your toes?"

He didn't budge.

The next day, when Miaomiao took Jordan out shopping, Anming sneaked into his son's room and stood by Michael Jordan's side. He regretted it right away and never did it again.

Since his twelfth birthday, Jordan began to take off, so to speak. A new mark was added to the Michael Jordan growth chart every month, if not every day. By his thirteenth birthday, Jordan had reached 150 cm. By his fourteenth birthday, which they celebrated only a month ago, Jordan had shot up to 165 cm. Anming didn't need the growth chart to tell him that his son was fast catching up with him in height. He could feel it everyday as Jordan swung his long arms and legs around in their small, low-ceiling two-and-a-half bedroom apartment.

"Pa," Jordan announced proudly, digging into a fat slice of his birthday cake. "Only two more centimeters and I'll be as tall as you are!"

Miaomiao's parents burst into a hearty laugh. Anming's parents laughed, too, but he sensed a bit of unease in their laugh. Did he imagine it? Had he noticed the same unease flitting across their eyes as they gazed at their only grandson lately?

Anming couldn't sleep well that night.

The rate at which Jordan was going, 10 to 15 cm a year, he would reach 185 cm by the time he was 16 years old. And he might continue to grow and gain a few more centimeters beyond that. 185 cm! Anming could picture that in his mind as if it had already happened. He could now lay to rest the worry that had been gnawing at him for so many years. He should be thrilled. He should feel proud. Vindicated. Instead he felt exactly like the time when he jumped to shoot a basket and the ball was knocked out of his hands by a much bigger, taller player from the other team. The guy's monstrously hard elbow hit his temple, too, and hit it hard.

He curled up in bed, wrapping his head tight in his hands.

Anming's own father—Jordan's paternal grandfather—was not tall. On Miaomiao's side, just about everybody in her family were of typical Chinese height, too. Those nutrition supplements had worked wonders as they had promised. He had read somewhere that genetics was a decisive factor in determining a child's physical as well as mental development. If that were true, why bother with nutrition and anything else? How tall was Michael Jordan's father? Anming didn't know. 167cm? That was impossible. Being an American, the lucky father must be at least 177 cm. But Michael Jordan was almost 200 cm. More than 20 cm taller than his father. Had his father ever lost sleep over this, too? What about Yao Ming? 230 cm! When he was first drafted by the Houston Rockets, a rumor went around in America that Yao Ming might have been a child of some bioengineering tricks in the lab. How could you otherwise explain so tall an athlete from China, a country known for a thousand other things, but not tall people?

But Yao Ming had his parents, both having played on national basketball teams, to thank for his height. Who should Jordan, *his* son, thank for his tallness gene? Him, his father? If not, who else?

"No! You turtle's son!" Anming cursed himself. "Don't even think that! Miaomiao chose *you*. Didn't she say she's yours, every ounce and centimeter of her?"

Even now, in her late 30s, Miaomiao could still turn heads in the streets. She giggled a lot when talking to her male colleagues in the Public Relations office. He could sense how they felt about her every time he went to her office.

But none of them was tall, or taller than 175 cm.

In fact, only a few people at the whole company were taller than 175 cm.

His basketball buddies.

The idea stunned him much worse than the monstrous elbow of some bully on the basketball court. He could feel a fire ravaging inside him from head to toe. He sat up in bed abruptly to remove his side of the quilt.

"Are you all right?" Miaomiao turned over and mumbled sleepily. He looked at her in the pale moonlight slanted through the window. How many times had he woke up in the middle of night before this night and reached to hold the full-length of this woman's soft, petite, well-curved body in his arms and felt so grateful and so aroused and so undeserving and so goddamm lucky? Yet he felt so sick tonight at the sight of her body. He lay down again and moved further to his side of the bed.

"It's nothing," he replied.

Tiezhu. Could it be him? They had been such pals since elementary school. He could trust just about everything to Tiezhu. No way. He had never seen anything untoward other than the occasional, friendly kind of banter between Tiezhu and Miaomiao. Well, they were such close friends. He was the same way with Yanyi, Tiezhu's wife, too, every now and again. What was the harm?

If he were to find anything tale-tell at all, Anming decided, he had to search hard in his memory about the days before Miaomiao rushed to the sink one early morning to throw up. That was so many years ago. Those days! What wouldn't he give to relive them! Except for the hours when she worked in the Public Relations office and he in the R & D department, they were like shadows to each other every day. They were such a pair of lovebirds.

About three months after their wedding Anming had to go to Tianjin for a week to be trained for a new test technology just imported from Germany. Even today he could still taste Miaomiao's salty tears as he kissed her goodbye at the train station, just like in the movies. That could have been the only window of opportunity. No. Miaomiao was not that kind of girl. She would never do anything like that. Never.

Yet how many times, when Jordan was small, had Tiezhu picked him up and teased: "Call me daddy!?"

Anming remembered feeling irritated by that kind of teasing and then annoyed with himself for having felt irritated.

Ever since that suspicion started to wriggle in his mind, it had been difficult for Anming to stay focused in bed.

"Don't worry." Miaomiao cooed in the darkness, understandingly, the first time he failed. "You've been working too hard lately. Something bothering you?"

He nodded, feeling ashamed.

"What's wrong?" Miaomiao sounded disappointed when he failed again a few days later. "Am I too old, not attractive to you any more?"

He shook his head. What else could he say?

"Perhaps you should go and see a doctor," Miaomiao murmured and rolled to her side of the bed.

Miaomiao hadn't tried again for two weeks now. How long could they last like that?

There was also Jordan's nose. It was much flatter than his.

Like a clove of garlic. Anming's nose was much better shaped: the bridge was firmer, the tip more pointed. Many a time Miaomiao had marveled when she nestled her head against his shoulder in front of the bedroom mirror:

"Just a few centimeters taller and you'd be the handsomest guy in the whole company!"

Where on earth did Jordan get that kind of nose? Poor kid. Everything else in his features was perfect. His grades were good, too.

"Where on earth!" Anming almost blurted out. He sighed.

"Aren't you going to get off?" the cab driver asked without looking back.

They were already outside the Number One Municipal Hospital. Anming paid and stepped out.

The hospital had just added a new wing of buildings: a twenty-floor main building plus several lower ones. The main building—with marble floors and huge windows, had four elevators in the hall, two on each side. It seemed everything had grown taller, bigger, and grander than when Jordan was born in this hospital.

Anming stepped into an elevator and pressed 15. When the door opened again, a thirtyish man pushed his way in before Anming was even half way out. Anming shot an angry glance backward and was about to mutter something when he noticed a short, pretty woman sniffling by the man's side, dabbing her tearful eyes with a handkerchief. Then the man and woman disappeared behind the elevator's stainless steel door.

Anming shook his head and trudged toward the suite at the other end of the hallway.

Several groups of people were already waiting there.

A young couple, in their late twenties perhaps, was sitting in a corner, the woman nursing the baby in her arms, the man staring ahead without blinking as if he were one of those new but so unsightly sculptures in the city park.

A man was hunched forward in a chair, his face buried deep in his palms. He was being treated to some rough talk by a middle-aged woman standing in front of him. The woman, somewhat tall and well dressed, kept pointing her index finger at the man's head to drive home whatever point she was making.

A young boy, about eight or nine years old, was chattering to an old couple, his grandparents perhaps. He looked like a bright kid and had a sunny smile on his face. A younger couple walked over and interrupted them, the man having a sheet of paper in his hands. The boy looked up, appeared to be frozen as if he suddenly realized something, and bolted. All four adults started to run after the boy, calling his name.

Anming dragged himself to the receptionist's window. Above was a sign that read: "GeneTreeChina"—in both Chinese and English. His legs trembled nervously.

"Name, please?" The young woman behind the window looked up and asked.

Anming fished out the receipt from underneath a picture of Jordan and his mother in his wallet and threw it over. He could hear his own breathing.

The woman turned to look among the envelopes in a big drawer next to her.

"Here we are," she said as her long, nimble fingers picked up an envelope. She pulled out the sheets inside, took a quick glance, and announced:

"1,999 *yuan* per test, 5,997 *yuan* altogether, minus the 1,000 *yuan* deposit, 4,997 *yuan* in balance."

That was equal to three months pay. But he had wanted to be absolutely sure with a triple-guarantee: hair, mouth swab, and blood tests.

"One kind of test would be enough. The accuracy rate is more than 99.99%!" the young woman had explained when he came to inquire three weeks ago.

Anming took out a bundle from the inner pocket of his jacket and passed it through the window. The money must still feel warm when the young woman counted it.

"Pa," Jordan had asked when Anming took him to the hospital for a physical two weeks ago. "Why bother?"

"Just to make sure you're as fit and strong as you look, you know," Anming lied. How else could he have managed with the mouth swab and the blood sample?

Now, the moment had come. The truth would put to rest all the cankerous worries that had been racking him day and night.

Anming stuffed the envelope in his pocket and hurried to the elevator area. Once inside an elevator, alone, he took out the envelope with trembling fingers and pulled out the sheets. He strained to read under the yellowish light from the glassy dome above. Before he could make sense of anything, however, the elevator had already reached the ground floor.

The door slid open.

The family he had seen earlier—the grandparents, the young couple, and the little boy, all five of them—were waiting down there, the boy's eyes still glistening with tears.

Why? Anming wondered. They had left something up there?

When he stepped out of the revolving doors of the main building, Anming's eyes were dazzled by the radiant sunshine sparkling in the world outside. Why hadn't he noticed it on his way to the hospital? He wondered. They couldn't have chosen a more perfect day for the championship game.

He stood there, as if not knowing where to go, and reached into his pocket to feel the hard-edged envelope between his fingers. Nurses, patients, and their families poured in and out of the revolving doors, casting curious glances at him.

He felt his fingers tightening their grip and, all of a sudden, crushing the envelope into a small, wrinkled ball.

He looked around. There was a trash bin in the form of a cute panda at the bottom of the long, front steps.

He took a deep breath, walked down the steps deliberately, stopped at about two meters away, took out the ball of crumpled paper, aimed, and shot the ball directly into the panda's mouth.

Hurrying out of the walled gate of the hospital, Anming felt the old spring bouncing in his legs again. What would it be like to play Michael Jordan, or Yao Ming, for that matter, one on one? Almost dizzied by the thought, Anming stepped right into the busy street to hail a cab. Several cars hit their brakes, honked, and their drivers stuck their heads out to cuss:

"Have you lost your head!?"

The Test *or* The Little Rice Wine Pot

Both sides outside the entrance of the county hospital were pulsating with life: florist stands with bucketfuls of chrysanthemums, roses, and evergreen leaves that looked disheartened under the early afternoon sun; greasy food tents filled with noisy diners and pungent aromas; peddlers sitting on the ground with dried roots displayed on dirty home-spun white cloth; tiny mice sprinting in perpetual circles on miniscule scales--one of the peddlers shrieking through a crackling boom box to curious passersby that his herbs could cure bronchitis, arthritis, prostatitis, infertility. . . and just about any other illness in the world.

She glanced at the small, makeshift tables arranged all around as Changsuo carried two big "sea bowls" of noodles toward her. The tables were all occupied. Many diners, busy working on the long, juicy noodles with their slender bamboo chopsticks, simply squatted wherever they could.

A middle-aged man sitting at a table next to her looked up from his noodles. His eyes fell on her belly and he scooted a few inches toward the diner on his right.

"Many thanks, big brother," she murmured, and sat down on the edge of the bench tentatively.

The mountainous noodles in the "sea bowl" on the table in

front of her looked soupy and appetizing with the fresh red chili sauce and a few pieces of fatty pork steak atop them, but she didn't feel like eating at all. Even though she had gone to the bathroom before leaving the hospital, she still felt full. She had drunk quite a bit of water before the test. The water hadn't gone through its natural cycle yet, and she was still somewhat dazed, her mind filled with that black and white, static blur pulsing on the screen.

She turned to look down at Changsuo squatting by her side. He was eating with gusto, producing a string of loud sucking, chewing noises. He must be starved after the long early morning bicycle ride from home to the county hospital, the anxious waiting outside the room before the test, and the test itself. His puffy, dark hair, unevenly parted in the middle, looked a bit messier than usual.

She picked up a piece of steak from her bowl and tried to place it in his. He jerked his upper body and the bowl to the other side, grunted, cast a quick, apologetic glance at the other diners around the small table (who were so busying themselves with their noodles that they didn't bother to raise their heads from their bowls), and shot her a stern "Why-don't-you-just-eat-woman?" stare.

Hypocrite! She smirked inwardly. If they were at home now, he would have said in a very tender voice: "Don't forget, you're eating for two people now."

The smirk on her lips faded when the thought came back again: Why couldn't she make any sense out of that blur pulsing on the screen?

She turned her eyes toward their Flying Dove bicycle rested against a huge willow tree on the other side of the cedar-padded road. Its gnarled, knotty trunk was so thick that it would probably take both her and Changsuo to lock their hands around it. Its several long, scraggly branches upheld an enormous leafy canopy for some of the florist stands, food tents, folk medicine peddlers, and whoever happened to be under its shade. It must be hundreds of years old, she guessed.

She saw something else not far from their bicycle: a tiny old woman huddling on the dirt ground, her bony hands reaching out with a small bowl, a ragged bundle and a feeble-looking stick by her side. A few loose gray hairs straggled on her small, leathery forehead and her closed eyes, her thin, toothless mouth murmuring sleepily without making any sound.

Why hadn't she noticed the old woman before?

She stood up, slowly, one palm on the tip of her protruding belly.

Changsuo looked up from his noodles and shot her another stare.

"I can't eat all of this," she mumbled. "It's too much."

Changsuo followed her eyes and saw the old woman under the tree, too.

"Woman, why don't you—" But Changsuo saw the look in her eyes and stopped before he could finish. He stood up, picked up her bowl, and made his way toward the old woman, and poured half of the noodles into her dusty bowl.

The old woman kowtowed several times, knocking her skinny forehead on the dirt ground, her toothless mouth quivering nervously with a flow of unintelligible babbling.

After that, she couldn't eat any more. She managed to take a few sips of the broth from her bowl but left the noodles untouched. Soon Changsuo was at the bottom of his bowl. Still sucking the residual flavor in his mouth noisily, he eyed her bowl on the table, but didn't say anything. At home, he would surely have urged her to eat, or would have simply picked up the bowl and finished whatever was left with a few quick, big mouthfuls.

Changsuo trudged toward their bicycle under the tree. His back, still young and strong, seemed hunched over just a little today, his left shoulder a bit higher than the right, as if he were burdened by a bag of corn or wheat seeds. When he was hunched over even just a little, Changsuo looked a lot like Pa, her father-in-law. Changsuo. Pa's only child.

She sighed.

The old woman stopped working on the noodles in her bowl and kowtowed again when Changsuo passed her to get the bicycle. How did she know it was him, ancient and half-blind as she was?

When they were just a few yards away from the noisy crowd outside the hospital and under the tree, Changsuo told her to sit on the bicycle's back seat first.

She flashed him a defiant, girlish smile, but kept on walking. Changsuo shook his head. As Changsuo and the bicycle started to roll smoothly, she quickened her steps, and, with her left hand on her belly, her right hand gripping the backseat frame, jumped. The bicycle shook with the impact, but Changsuo stabilized it quickly.

They were on their way home.

She couldn't get it out of her head: that black-and-white blur on the screen. She wondered again as they left behind the busy, tree-lined streets and embarked on the ten-mile-long cedar-padded trek back to Wu Village. Why couldn't she make any sense out of it?

"See? You see that? That's the heartbeat," the fiftyish half-bald technician at the hospital had said, matter-of-factly, as his sinewy hand moved the cold metal piece on her belly.

"You see it, woma—Yingzi?" Changsuo exclaimed tremulously by the bedside. She could feel the dampness in his tight, nervous hand grasping hers.

Yes, she could see it. A new life was pulsing on the screen right up there, a new life coming from her, from her man, and from her and her man together. In a few more months she would be a mother. Imagine that! No, in fact she was already a mother. She had been a mother ever since that monthly nuisance in her body hadn't come as expected about six months back.

"No," the technician moved the cold metal piece on her belly a few more times, as if to make sure, and announced. "No. I don't see any soybeans."

What did he mean? She didn't understand. What did the man mean?

"What do you mean?" Changsuo asked nervously. He stood up abruptly, letting go of her hand, and craned his neck to get a closer look at the screen. "What soybeans? Try again! I beg you. . . ."

"If you can't see a pair of soybeans," the technician stood up to point at a spot on the screen, "right there, it means. . . ."

But what *did* he mean? She didn't understand.

She and Changsuo had been very careful. They had waited for a perfect time not to use any protection: A beautiful full moon coinciding with the first day her body was clean again. She was thinking of Weiwei, her elder brother's fat, rose-cheeked baby son, the whole time. She had craved for sour things, pickled cucumbers, turnips, onions, as if she couldn't have enough.

"When I was carrying Changsuo," her mother-in-law had said, beaming joyously, "sour things were all I craved for months."

Everybody said she glowed radiantly as her body began to show. Changsuo would marvel every night, holding her face gently between his big, callused palms when the two were in the privacy of their own room:

"You've turned into a real fairy, woman!"

When had he started calling her "woman" instead of her name, Yingzi? The morning after their wedding night?

Then, everybody said she was carrying low, very low.

Even Lan, the village doctor who had arranged for the test through her contacts at the county hospital, had been upbeat when she felt Yingzi's pulse:

"Very strong, assertive, not timid at all."

And she had been focusing her thoughts on Weiwei all the time, all the way to the county hospital, up till the moment she stepped into the test room.

So much for all the hope the whole family had placed on her.

But what had gone wrong? What if that machine was broken? Why hadn't she protested and asked for another test? She wouldn't have been able to make any sense, though, puzzled as she was by those ominous-looking machines she had caught glimpses of while treading through the hallways of the hospital.

She sighed. Her legs had gone asleep and her bottom felt prickly numb. She waited until a loud, puttering tractor had caught up and passed by before shifting her position, ever so slightly, on the small, hard back seat.

"You okay? Want me to stop and take a rest?" Changsuo asked, pedaling breathily.

"No. We'll be home soon."

She put her right arm around Changsuo's waist, like in the old days when they were still dating, and rested her cheek against his back. She could feel her man's tensed muscles. She could hear his heart beat, loud, clear, and vigorous. For generations her man's family line had been carried on, rather precariously, by the heartbeat of an only male child like Changsuo. How odd.

"Changsuo?"

"Huh?"

"Nothing."

Two hours later, their Flying Dove was bumping along the narrow, mud road inside Wu Village. It looked the same as they had left it early in the morning, when it was still drowsing in a thin, dusky haze. The same houses. The same trees. A few small boys and girls were playing glass ball and jumping rope on the threshing ground. Changsuo didn't ring the bell on the hand bar loud and clarion-like as he used to when they passed by the kids playing.

Ma was waiting outside their home, squinting, her right hand shielding her eyes against the dazzling glory of the setting sun.

"Ma," Changsuo said as he stopped, balanced the bicycle with his feet on the ground, and dismounted. Then, one hand holding the handlebar, one hand supporting his wife, he helped her dismount.

"Ma," Yingzi said as she tried hard to stand on her feet. They were so prickly, painfully gone.

Ma hurried over and gave her daughter-in-law her rough,

callused hand.

"You must be very tired, Yingzi," Ma said with a smile, eyes fixed on her face, but darting away instantly.

"I'm okay, Ma."

As she and Ma stepped into the cement-floored family room, she heard Changsuo mumbling something to Pa, who was hunching at the dining table, the cigarette in his mouth having burnt almost to its butt. Apparently Pa had come home from the fields quite a bit earlier than usual.

"Pa," she cooed softly.

"Mmmm, you're back." Pa's gray-haired head looked up and nodded.

Pa already knew. Otherwise, his eyes would be glittering with joy, his many-lined face blossoming radiantly, revealing the few heavily-stained teeth still remaining in his mouth. Simple and of few words, Pa had been kind to his daughter-in-law.

When she came out again from their own room, Pa, Ma, and Changsuo were waiting for her at the dining table. Ma had prepared a small feast for the occasion: a big pot of whole chicken soup, a plate of steamed salted fish, and a stir-fry of tomato, green pepper, and eggs—her favorite vegetable dish.

Ma stood up, got hold of a big, meaty chicken leg between her chopsticks and placed it in her daughter-in-law's bowl, and added a few ladles of rich broth, black mushrooms, and baby bamboo slices.

"You must be starved," Ma said, grinning. "When I was carrying Changsuo, I had such a good appetite all the time."

Changsuo picked up a tall white porcelain pot and poured some rice wine into a small cup for Pa and into another for himself. The pot had a long, curving spout.

Yeah, she should eat even though the life she was carrying inside her would not grow a little wine pot between the legs. Still, she must eat for the two of them.

She had a sip of the soup. It was so delicious. Feeling a pang of hunger, she began to eat with gusto as Pa and Changsuo, and occasionally Ma, chatted on and off, about what was happening in the county and what had happened in Wu Village while they were away.

When supper was over, Pa left to feed the pigs in the sty, Changsuo went to check the small Wu Village Handcraft Shop he was managing. She offered to help Ma clear the table and clean the dishes, but Ma insisted she retire to her room to rest.

"Your legs must be swollen. When I was carrying Changsuo. . . ."

Finally she was in her own room—her and Changsuo's room. She sat down in a cushioned willow chair and stretched out her legs. They were not swollen, but they weren't in the best shape either.

She picked up the remote control on the nightstand by her side and aimed it at the 19-inch Panda color TV set atop the dresser. Instead of the black and white, soybean-less image flashing on the screen, she saw a group of gray-haired retirees doing taiji exercises in a park.

The TV set was a wedding gift from her own parents when she married. What would her own Pa and Ma say when they knew the test result? She wondered. Lingzi, her brother's wife, didn't give birth to Weiwei until her third try. Each of the first two times when she came back from the county hospital, Lingzi looked so crushed, like a big, overripe tomato that had been stamped upon brutally.

"Sis," Lingzi would murmur weakly, holding the slender hand of her sister-in-law, still a maiden then. "The way they slid that cold metal thing in and snuffed the life out of me! It hurt so much I would rather have died myself."

The third time, when the midwife held the freshly born bundle of pink flesh to show her the tiny, wrinkled wine pot between a pair of little legs, Lingzi cried and laughed so hard, almost hysterically.

"No," Yingzi mumbled to herself as she stared at the TV screen blankly. She would rather die than let herself go through that. When the test was over this morning, the half-bald technician had suggested, as if it were an afterthought, that he could "make arrangements" for a very small referral fee. She pretended not to hear and led Changsuo out of the room.

Changsuo. What was it like when he was born? Pa and Ma, and their Pa and Ma must have laughed and cried with tears in their eyes, too, when they saw what was hanging between his little legs. Unlike today, they had had no way of really knowing in advance, had they?

She shook her head.

Without any cable—she had heard that with cable, city folks could watch just about anything they wanted to—the Panda set didn't offer many stations for her to choose from. The picture was clear one minute and blurry, as if it were snowing, the next, but that didn't matter much. Anything that could take her mind off whatever was on her mind would be fine.

She pressed the remote in her hand. A meteorologist dressed in red shirt and white jacket was forecasting tomorrow's temperatures at the major cities around the country.

She pressed again. An elderly actor donning a painted face,

a chest-long beard, and a colorful Beijing Opera costume, having worked a note to a sky-high pitch, held it up there for a long, long time before bringing it down to earth again, all in one breath, winning thunderous applause from the audience.

With another press on the remote, more than a dozen grinning foreigners, little babies in arms, rambled toward her on the screen. A young reporter's voice narrated off-screen that these "golden-haired, blue-eyed" Americans (even though several from the group appeared to be dark-haired, and gray-eyed, she thought) had just adopted from a municipal orphanage; the happy parents were taking their new daughters for a quick sightseeing tour before returning to their home country.

The mothers of those baby girls. How would they feel if they happened to be watching the same program she was watching now? Could any of them recognize her own daughter, her own flesh and blood, she would never see again?

Yingzi remembered another news story not too long ago about a Buddha-hearted Fujian businessman who had adopted hundreds of orphans, mostly girls, some seriously handicapped. One of the girls, when he found her in the roadside bushes, was almost dead, her face having been stung swollen by ants and flies.

How would that baby girl's mother feel if she knew what had happened?

And Changsuo. He hadn't said a word yet. What was he thinking now?

Yingzi didn't know when she dozed off in the chair, and when Changsuo came back he carried her onto their bed.

One day, about three months later, while she was helping

Pa and Ma fertilize wheat seedlings in the field, she felt a sudden, tearing pain in her belly. The pain persisted. Her water broke, too.

"Old man, go get Lan, and Changsuo! Hurry!" Ma shouted to Pa while grabbing her daughter-in-law's arms to give her support. "Yingzi, it'll be all right. When I was having . . . ."

Several hours later, after so much pushing, moaning, screaming, and clawing at Changsuo's hand and whatever was within reach by the bedside, the new life inside her body was born. Lan, the village doctor, held the bundle of freshly born pink flesh in front of her and cooed:

"Meet Mama, and Papa!"

No miracle had happened. There was no wrinkled little rice wine pot between the baby's little legs. It was so flat there. Yet the baby looked so healthy, so beautiful, so like the best of her and Changsuo put together.

Tears welled in her eyes. She turned to look at Changsuo. He smiled back. There were tears in his eyes, too.

Life had gone on as before since they came back from the county hospital. Except that Changsuo had been much quieter. The whole family had been much quieter. Yingzi herself hadn't been her usual happy, chatty self, either.

One evening, though, when a big, golden moon was hanging low outside their window, Changsuo picked up his *erhu* that had been hanging on the wall untouched for months, sat by the window, and began to play.

As his quivering fingers moved up and down the two strings, the bow weaved left and right and bounced rhythmically, she saw herself and Changsuo walking in the cornfields again, tipsy like, under a vast, moonlit evening sky; the tense, trembling arm of the young man, emboldened by her head brushing against his shoulder as they wandered around, encircling her slender waist for the first time; her blushing face being cupped in a pair of strong palms, her eyes looking into a pair of wild, fiery eyes whose fire could only be put out with fire. . . .

Suddenly, the *erhu* began to speak in a different voice, a deeper, sadder, much older voice, the voice of an ancient, blind minstrel wandering alone between heaven and earth. Then everything became a blur.

She was bewildered and couldn't make out the blur she was seeing.

"Changsuo," she murmured when he stopped playing.

"Huh?" Changsuo said, replacing the *erhu* on the wall.

"What are you thinking?"

"Nothing."

"Tell me, Changsuo, like in the old days."

"Nothing, really," Changsuo sighed, sat by the bedside, and held her hand. Then he added, as if it had just occurred to him: "Remember the old woman, alone, under the tree outside the hospital?"

She now knew what she was seeing while listening to Changsuo playing. In that same picture was another face, tiny, swollen with insect bites.

Now that the fresh, new life had finally arrived, there was a lot more noise and activity in the house though the sound could be a bit heartier, less subdued.

The first time she placed the tip of her swollen breast into the baby's small, toothless mouth, she felt tickled. The baby sucked, released the teat, and cried as if it had been deceived.

"Changsuo?" Ma called, then whispered to her daughter-in-law, "I remember the first time I suckled Changsuo. . . ."

"What is it, Ma?" Changsuo stepped in from the family room.

"The baby needs you," Ma stepped out, smiling.

"Me?" Changsuo sounded incredulous when he realized what was expected of him.

She blushed, flashed him a funny look, and giggled.

Changsuo shot a quick, sheepish glance at the door, squatted down, and placed his big, vigorous mouth around her teat and sucked.

That was the best moment in her life for a long, long time.

Ma had once told her that to give their only child a boost, she had nursed Changsuo until he was too old to do so in public. They had also dressed him like a girl until he was ten years old.

"Why?" Yingzi, not yet Ma's daughter-in-law then, asked even though she already knew the answer.

"So that he had a chance to grow up, you know. The Devil wouldn't be too interested in taking away the life of a cheap girl."

It was quite a ceremony when the barber came to cut off Changsuo's long pigtail on his tenth birthday. They had three tables of relatives and neighbors to come and help celebrate.

When Yingzi teased him about it on one of their moonlit night walks outside, Changsuo was so annoyed and didn't want to talk about it at all. After all, it had taken him years to shake off the "sissy" reputation that had chased him around at school and on the threshing ground.

Changsuo had wanted to leave Wu Village and seek fortune elsewhere, in one of those booming coastal cities, but Pa and Ma didn't want to hear about it. They would rather be dirt poor and live on northwest wind than see their only child go out of their sight.

Would she and Changsuo let their son go out and see the world for himself? She would. Changsuo would. Probably.

"What are you talking about, woman?" she could imagine Changsuo shooting her an impatient, incredulous stare.

Right, what was she thinking about? That question wouldn't even apply to them because the baby she was holding in her arms and was suckling this very moment didn't have a little rice wine pot growing between the legs.

One evening, while nursing the baby in her own room, she overheard Changsuo talking with Pa and Ma in their room on the other side of the family room.

"I can't do that," Changsuo sounded upset. "Yingzi. She—"

Pa and Ma sighed.

"It's up to you," Pa mumbled. "Your ma and I have you, but who is going to pour wine for you in your old age? Huh?"

"What is it?" she asked when Changsuo came back to their room.

"Nothing," he shook his head.

When she got up to nurse the baby well past midnight, Changsuo was still wide-awake, his eyes fixed on the ceiling blankly.

"I know what you're thinking." She trembled, shocked by her own voice in the deadly quiet night.

Changsuo turned his head and gazed at her. Then, he got up, sat next to her, and held her waist with his long, strong arm. They both turned to look at the baby at her breast.

The baby had a well-shaped forehead and a head of shiny, black hair. Her little eyebrows, nose, and mouth were all clear, clean, and curved vividly. She would be prettier than her mama when she grew up and more intelligent than her papa.

Changsuo reached to touch the baby's face tenderly. A teardrop fell on the back of his own hand.

On the tenth day after the baby was born, there was a quiet celebration. Yingzi's mother, younger sister, sister-in-law, and Weiwei, arrived close to noon with gifts of cute, fluffy baby clothes, two chickens, a basket of eggs, dried nuts, brown sugar, and whatnot.

"Congratulations, Sis," her mother enthused to Ma, when she stepped inside the house.

"Oh, I should congratulate you instead, Sis," Ma beamed, grasping her in-law's free hand warmly, "you have such good fortune!"

Lingzi told her two-year-old son, still in her arms, to greet Pa: "Call Grandpa!"

Weiwei stared at Pa timidly and jerked his head away.

"It's okay," Pa grinned with an awkward smile and pretended to pinch Weiwei's nose with his fingers. "One day Grandpa will have a fat little devil like you, too, right?"

They all roared with a hearty laugh.

Then they came to her room to see the baby. Everybody marveled how pretty and healthy and adorable the baby was.

The newly-minted maternal Grandma made some funny, snappy noise with her tongue to tease the baby, then picked her up, and held her in her arms: "Oh, my little precious. My little precious."

Yingzi saw her mother's eyes well up.

The first opportunity they had a private moment together, Lingzi lowered her voice and asked,: "You're all right, Yingzi?"

She nodded. What could be wrong with her, anyway?

Late in the afternoon, her mother and her entourage got up to leave. They had lots of things to attend to at home on the other side of the hill.

"Yingzi," her mother said before leaving, holding her daughter's hand, "you're so fortunate, you know. Everybody's been so kind to you."

That day it was her turn to stare at the ceiling blankly till hours past midnight. Changsuo asked, sleepy-eyed, when he got up to pee: "What is it, woma—Yingzi?"

She didn't answer.

On the fifteenth day after the baby was born, she and Changsuo got up at around three o'clock in the morning. She suckled the baby first, carefully placed on her chest a slip of paper she had written and torn and rewritten many times: "Laidi. Born . . ."

She wrapped the baby up warmly in a small floral quilt she had made herself. In a small bag was stuffed a few articles of clothing for Laidi—meaning "beckoning in a little brother"—and a tiny mosquito net.

With Laidi in her arms, she tiptoed behind Changsuo, who was carrying the bicycle out so that it wouldn't make any noise. From Pa and Ma's room came a cough. It was Pa. She stopped and turned to look. The house was deadly quiet again. She lifted the corner of the quilt shielding the baby's face: Laidi was soundly asleep, too.

She stepped out and shuddered when a chilly breeze greeted her face. While Changsuo balanced the bicycle with his feet on the ground, she managed to sit on the small, hard back seat first, then adjusted her position so that she could hold Laidi with the left arm and grip the seat frame with her right hand.

They were on their way.

The houses, trees, and fields alongside the narrow dirt road were still covered by a thin layer of wispy fog. Occasionally a dog barked, and a rooster crowed. Otherwise, the two-hour ride to the county was like a freefall into a cold, bottomless hole.

Light was breaking but the sky was still hazy when they arrived. They passed through tree-lined streets, the huge construction site for the new county government compound, the town square packed with old and new stores. . . .

She didn't know why Changsuo didn't stop at any one of these places. She was still dizzy from the freefall.

Then, she knew, vaguely, where Changsuo was going.

Finally, Changsuo stopped, balanced the bicycle with his feet on the ground, and helped her dismount. As she followed Changsuo toward the enormous, gnarled, knotted willow tree outside the county hospital, she noticed a blurry bundle, with a stick by its side, under the tree. It was covered by frost, too. She shivered.

Where they were standing would be a perfect spot. It would be bustling with life in an hour or two, like they had seen months ago.

Gently, she laid the bundle in her arms on the ground, lifted the corner of the quilt for one last look and covered it again, pulled out the tiny mosquito net from the bag, spread it over the little bundle, and placed little pebbles around the edges to hold it down.

When she straightened her back, Changsuo was looking in the opposite direction, as if he had nothing to do with what was happening at all. He was ready to leave.

Her mind was still in that numb, half-asleep kind of state as she climbed on the back seat and Changsuo began pedaling through the still empty, tree-lined streets in town.

It was over, finally. She—they—had to start all over again. But what could they do to guarantee that they'd succeed the second time? The dried roots and leaves that loud, foamy peddler displayed on that dirtied white cloth on the ground? She would rather throw her money into the Twin-Sun River than. . . .

Suddenly, she heard a loud cry piecing the early morning quiet. The cry persisted. It came from a house they had just passed. Then came a soothing voice trying to comfort the baby. The baby whined a bit more, then stopped crying; it's mama had stuffed her teat into the baby's mouth.

The Flying Dove had stopped, too, and stopped so suddenly that she hit her head hard against Changsuo's back. The bike skipped, shuddered, and balanced precariously on two wheels, as if frozen in time; then turned around, and started to go—to fly—in the direction it has just come from. Changsuo pedaled so hard that he was hunched over the handle bars.

Yingzi placed her cheek against his back—the first time she had touched him for days—and felt the tensed muscles underneath his jacket.

"Hurry!" she screamed, hysterically, raining blows on his back with her fist.

"You Big Sissy! You heartless, spineless turtle's son!"

Teacher Yu

I had meant to go and see my middle school language teacher for years, but every time I visited China, I'd be flying between Shanghai, Shenzhen, Beijing, and Hong Kong, hammering out deals between my company and Chinese enterprises hungry for foreign investments and technical know-how, then hopping on the first flight available back to my family in Westchester, NY, much in the fashion of Henry Kissinger in the heyday of his shuttle diplomacy.

When Kissinger was secretly arranging for Nixon's historic visit to Beijing, I was still a dim-witted kid perched on the threshold of pubescence. Our school, which happened to be surrounded by crowded alleys, small mills, and sewage ditches, was still teeming with wild weeds, but we were back in the classrooms to thumb through books and tamper with factors and Newton's laws of motion.

The use of plural for "book" was uncalled for, though, as far as our language class was concerned because we had only one textbook: the Little Red Book. By middle school, even the dumbest among us could recite, almost verbatim, its content from page one all the way to page 270. We had been breathing it in like air for so long and we couldn't have dodged it even in our dreams.

When the fall semester began and our new language teacher

walked in with that familiar pocket-sized red book in hand, we—about thirty of us squeezed in the brick-floored classroom—knew we were in for another round of tireless lectures of the earth-shattering significance of the Great Leader's quotations and endless confessions of the first hint of selfish thoughts that dared to flit across the recesses of our little minds.

Our new teacher, medium height, late thirties, had a head of fluffy, shiny hair combed smoothly all the way to the back. It looked so cool, so stylish. My own hair, to say the least, was unruly and hugged my adolescent scalp just a bit too intimately for my comfort.

The teacher picked up a piece of chalk and wrote his name on the blackboard:

Jiye Yu

Jiye meant carrying on the great cause. Teacher Yu had just been transferred to our school thanks to a knee injury he had suffered as a geologist cracking rocks in the mountains.

Having introduced himself, Teacher Yu got down to business right away.

"Open your book to page one. 'The force at the core leading our cause forward is. . . .'"

Sitting upright on our stools with the Little Red Book held at an arm's length, we began to shout in our tuneless singsong voices:

"The force at the core leading our cause forward is. . . ."

Half way through the long quotation: "It is an arduous task to ensure a better life for the several hundred million people of China and to build our economically and culturally backward country into a prosperous and powerful one with a high level of culture. . ." a few pages later, we felt tired, thirsty, and restless.

Taozi, sitting to my left, took out his new fountain pen and began to draw on the desk we were sharing between us. The surface of the wooden desk was still scarred with "Down with" this and "Down with" that, such fiery revolutionary slogans carved in with pencil knives. As Taozi's pen moved expertly on the desk, the shape of a pretty girl appeared. She had a nice, oval face, a pair of disproportionately big eyes and her long, thick braids dangled tantalizingly on her chest. Taozi paused for a second, as if hesitating, then added a curly moustache between her pointed nose and pouting lips.

I fished out a small, palm-sized mirror from my pocket to be shielded by the Little Red Book and tilted it toward Meiling who was sitting at a desk to my right. Starting from spring Meiling began to look noticeably different. The skin in her face softened and assumed a faint rosy kind of tone. Her eyes, more vivid, would cast themselves downward, shyly, whenever they met mine accidentally. Her body? Well, I was frankly clueless about what was going on with her body. All I knew was that whenever my eyes glanced at her chest—which looked even curvier and more ample with that new, well-fitting, light blue blouse she had on for the first day of school—I would feel something rushing to my head.

I could see Meiling's face in the mirror now, her eyes, her nose, and the small birthmark right above her right upper lip. A faint smile appeared around her lips as she flashed a quick, shy glance in my direction.

Suddenly I felt the absence of the teacher's voice in the listless drone in the classroom. I looked up and met Teacher Yu's eyes. Being one of the shortest in the class, I had the dubious honor of sitting in the front row close to the teacher's lectern. I could even smell whiffs of tobacco in the air as Teacher Yu paced in front of the class with the Little Red Book between his nicotine-stained fingers. Had he noticed what I was doing, the new braids Taozi was adding to the poor girl's head, and whatever tricks those sitting behind me were all up to?

"All right, let's shift gears and read something different," Teacher Yu announced after he shut his Little Red Book and placed it back on the lectern.

He picked up a piece of chalk and started to write on the blackboard. We all remained quiet as the tip of the chalk danced scratchily across the roughly painted cement surface:

Tsiek tsiek and again tsiek tsiek,
Mulan weaves, facing the door.
You don't hear the shuttle's sound,
You only hear Daughter's sighs.
They ask Daughter who's in her heart,
They ask Daughter who's on her mind. . . .

When there was no more space on the board for him to write, Teacher Yu turned around, clapped his hands to get rid of the chalk dust on his fingers, and began to read aloud, his head swaying this way and that way, his big Adam's apple moving up and down rhythmically, in perfect resonance with the flow of the lines.

For the first time I noticed that Teacher Yu's voice was so soothing, so lute-like. It sounded so pleasant to the ear.

I turned to check on Taozi, my desk mate, who had abandoned the poor nymph on the desk reluctantly. He had looked so enraptured.

I stole a glance at Meiling. There was such a dreamy look in her eyes as they fixed on Teacher Yu's face, and her lips half opened as if her whole being were being drawn out into the air from deep inside her.

The next day, Teacher Yu handed out a copy of the complete Mulan poem in his forceful handwriting. The dark green ink on the rough, grayish paper it was printed on had not completely dried yet. As I joined the invigorated chorus in the classroom, I could picture the homecoming of a young woman warrior who had gone to war in her father's stead: She removed her wartime gown, put on her old, girly clothes, fixed her cloudlike hair with a mirror, and reappeared in front of her comrades-in-arms who hadn't had a clue that their young, handsome general was actually a beautiful woman.

If Meiling were to pull that kind of stunt on me, I wondered, could I be fooled? Meiling's soft skin, her giggling voice, and her shapely body, would have betrayed her, I figured. If I had gone to fight wars, and returned ten years later, would Meiling be still waiting for me? Waiting for *me*! We hadn't even exchanged a word about anything yet!

Soon it became a kind of understanding, an open secret between Teacher Yu and us young pupils that for each class we would spend the first ten to fifteen minutes reading aloud—so loud that even those in the central building would be able to hear us—from the Little Red Book, and for the rest of the class we would read Li Po or Tu Fu from *Three Hundred Tang Poems*, or even a piece from *Best Essays from Antiquity*. Teacher Yu would chuckle and sigh as he led us in reading Li Po's poem on drinking alone under the moon and dancing with the moon and the poet's own shadow. His eyes glistened and his voice quivered as he reached the end of Tu Fu's poem on his thatched hut being blown away by furious, wet wind:

If I could get a mansion with a thousand, ten thousand rooms,
I'd give all poor, homeless scholars joy and shelter from cold.
Solid as a mountain, the elements could not move it.
Oh! If I could see this mansion before me,
I'd happily freeze to death in my broken hut!

A few weeks into the semester, Mr. Liu, Director of the Revolutionary Committee, and *de facto* principal of the school, came to our class. With a crew cut and visible cheekbones in his skinny face, Director Liu looked rather stern.

"It has come to my attention," he said, "that some teachers are resurrecting old feudal, bourgeois weeds to poison the minds of our pupils." His voice sounded paper thin, even shrill. "I warn you to maintain your revolutionary vigilance so as not to be corrupted."

I now knew that something was afoot. I mean Taozi, Meiling, and the whole class knew it. Yet Teacher Yu went ahead with what he was doing as if he didn't know or just didn't give one iota about it all.

"Now, it's time for *us* to learn to write," Teacher Yu said one afternoon when we had read a few pages from the Little Red Book. "The topic for our first essay assignment is—" he coughed suddenly. The outburst caused his head of shiny hair to bounce uneasily. After blowing his nose with a large handkerchief, he continued: "'Study Hard for the Revolution.'"

Half drowsed by cicadas chirping shrilly among the tree tops in the school yard as if to rival the muffled voices of a man and a woman broadcasting the latest Mao quotation from a loudspeaker in the alley outside, I told myself to give my best with the assignment. To please Teacher Yu, perhaps.

The next day I handed in the fruit of my labor with an I-hope-you'll-like-it kind of smirk in my face.

My essay began with a grand, oratorical sweep about the Five Continents and Four Oceans trembling with the good tidings of revolutions, which sent echoes across the 9,600,000 square kilometers of the motherland, which was being graced by red flags waving high and fluttering in gusty winds, which carried more good tidings to the province, the city, and all the way down to our middle school, before it winded down to a declaration that we the young pupils should. . . .

"Look, I'm not so sure about this continents and oceans business," Teacher Yu tapped my masterpiece with his tobacco-stained fingers before handing it back to me a couple of days later. "I'd prefer *kai men jian shan.*" Seeing the mountain after pushing open the door. It was classic advice about being direct in essay-writing.

Crestfallen, I went about cutting the continents and oceans (to please Teacher Yu, perhaps), and returned, the next morning, with a clean copy of the revised essay for the teacher in his office.

Teacher Yu took a quick look and nodded. Not a single hair fell loose from his clean, well-combed head. "Mmmm, better, but I still can't see the mountain right away."

I went back and cut and trimmed more until all the flags

and good tidings had been thrown out. All I had left was clean, wide open space before the mountain, a silly, nonsensical five-paragraph thing at the best, but it was my first real essayistic attempt.

Sitting in his squeaky chair at his desk, Teacher Yu nodded with a smile on his face.

I had meant to warn him about Director Liu, but chickened-out because two other teachers were also in the small, crowded office.

Last summer, I flew to Guangzhou to arrange for a joint pharmaceutical company there to send 50 of its technicians to the U.S. to be trained at Boehringer Ingelheim in Danbury, CT. Everything went so smoothly that when I stuffed all the signed documents in the briefcase, I still had two days left before my scheduled flight back to New York. I rushed to the White Cloud Airport and hopped on the first available flight to Nanjing, where I was born and went to school until I had to move away with my family. I was more than determined than ever to see Teacher Yu this time.

Nanjing, a two-thousand-year-old city, had metamorphosed into something so modern, so eerily alien that I could barely recognize it as my birthplace, my first hometown.

"Are you sure this is it?" I asked before stepping out of the taxi.

"Is there another school by the same name around here?" The young driver gave me a look while handing me the change.

I stood in front of a gate wide enough for two cars to go in abreast of each other. A big glossy marble sign under the arched portal read:

Nanjing No. 48 Municipal Middle School

Inside the gate was a campus alive with lush green grass, young pines, cherries, and chrysanthemums, new multi-level buildings of contemporary design, and high-pitched choruses of students practicing English after their teachers.

Could this be the same school I attended 30 years ago?

I strolled around the campus desperately looking for something that could, even remotely, connect me with this place, now surrounded by residential complexes filled with tall, glassy, red-roofed buildings. It looked so arbitrary under a cloudless early June sky.

I found it.

Huddling in the back of the campus, right behind the new, seven-story Central Building was an old, small, two-story structure. The white paint on its walls had chipped off and revealed underneath a fiery revolutionary slogan in deep red paint. What looked like a warehouse now or an eyesore to be knocked down any day to make room for a new tennis court used to be the power center of my middle school. On its wall a senseless kid had stuck a big-character poster that started a storm and changed the life of its writer and the lives of several others.

One day, about two months into that fall semester 30 years ago, Teacher Yu failed to show up for the scheduled class. A few minutes after the bell stopped ringing, Director Liu hurried into our room to make an announcement.

"Teacher Yu has committed serious errors and is under investigation." Liu's thin voice sounded scratchier than usual. "The school's Revolutionary Committee has decided that I will teach your language class instead. For the time being."

I was shocked. So were Taozi, Meiling, and the rest of the class.

Director Liu opened his Little Red Book with trembling fingers and got down to business right away.

Again we thumbed through the pages of the Little Red Book and droned on and on, in our tuneless singsong voices, what we could recite even in our sleep.

After class, I hurried to the central building to look for Teacher Yu in his office. He wasn't there.

I went from building to building and looked through the windows of every room and finally found him in a small room in a low building in the back of the school yard.

A silhouetted figure of Teacher Yu was sitting at an old table near a window at the other end of the room. On the table was a stack of paper and a fountain pen. Behind him was a bare, single cot. He was looking outside his window, apparently in deep thought. A cigarette was left burning between his fingers.

I tapped on the window at my end and called in a hushed voice:

"Teacher Yu?"

He turned, looked surprised, and then smiled awkwardly.

"Are you all right?" I asked.

He nodded and smiled again. Then he waved me to leave, took a drag at the cigarette, and turned his gaze back to outside his window.

The next morning, while horsing around before class, we saw a woman coming into the school with a small bundle: a blanket, simple clothing, and what looked like a few toiletries. Director Liu came out of his office and took the woman to the back of the school yard. She was very good looking and had an air of gracefulness in her movement, but her head was hanging low on her chest.

Later that day we were told that Teacher Yu would not be allowed to go home until he had confessed and repented all of his egregious errors.

After school, I went straight to the stationery store a few streets from my home and bought two sheets of white paper, a writing brush, and a bottle of black ink.

The next morning, a big-character poster appeared on the wall of the central building, right next to Director Liu's office. Its bold title in a young adolescent's uneven brushwork questioned:

What Crime Is It to Teach the Classics?

The big-character poster, actually a mini-essay, with page after page stuck to the wall, opened with a brief description of what had happened to Teacher Yu, which was followed with a statement that the writer, as a young Red Guard of Chairman Mao, didn't think that classics such as Li Po and Tu Fu were feudal, bourgeois weeds because they sang the sorrows of the common people and their heroism in the face of foreign aggression, and because they were so beautifully written and sounded so much like music to the ear. It ended with this question: How could we hope to build our country into "a prosperous and powerful one with a high level of culture," as our Great Leader Chairman Mao himself envisioned, without teaching the younger generation the best our culture had to offer?

As I watched, from some distance, a big crowd gathering in

front of the poster, I was shaking with nervous excitement.

Taozi elbowed out of the crowd and walked over to me. "Why didn't you tell me? I could've signed on it, too!"

Meiling was also in the crowd. She turned and gave me a shy glance. All the risk that I had imagined I was taking while sticking the poster to the wall now seemed worth it.

By the end of the third class that morning, a sudden chill descended on the whole school. Three or four important-looking people from the district had arrived in a Beijing jeep, one of them in deep blue police uniform. They stood in front of the poster for a long while, pointing at this line and that line, the police officer taking a few snapshots, then disappeared behind the door of Director Liu's office.

Half an hour later, Director Liu came to our classroom. As I was leaving my desk to follow him to his office, I felt the eyes of the whole class on my back. My legs were shaking weakly.

All eyes of the officials from the district shot to the door as I stepped into Director Liu's office, and searched in my face greedily as if they couldn't wait to swallow me up whole.

"Why did you write that rubbish?" A half-bald official sitting at a desk in the middle of the room glared at me and roared.

I tried to say something, but couldn't find my voice.

"Who is behind this?" snapped the police officer, his rice-grain-size small eyes glued to my face.

"No one," I mumbled, looking down at the brick floor.

"Liar!" Director Liu bolted up in his chair. "You're just a dumb little kid. Even in your dreams you couldn't have cooked up something like that!"

"It *was* me, and me alone," I murmured again, lifting my head to look into the eyes of the officials.

The room fell into a silence.

"What's your father's class?" asked the half-bald official as he fell back in his chair, letting out a loud awkward squeak. He was drumming a black-covered notebook with his fingers impatiently.

"Proletariat."

The official turned to Director Liu, who nodded slightly.

"Your grandfather's?"

"Proletariat. Revolutionary martyr," I replied proudly.

All four district officials turned to Director Liu, who shook his head as if he couldn't believe it either, then nodded again.

"And your great-grandfather's?"

The interrogation went on for a few more minutes when the half-bald official whispered with the others in the room, coughed loudly to clear his throat, and delivered the verdict:

"You should thank your lucky stars that you were born in such a red family, son. Otherwise your sorry ass would begin to rot in jail starting from this very day! Now, we don't want to see your face again in this school until you have repented. . . ."

For the next few days I bit the tip of my fountain pen in my room at home and couldn't find anything to put down on paper that would be worthy of the eyes of Director Liu and those district officials.

My parents were devastated. At supper Pa would grunt through his nose every now and then and sigh, Ma would dab her eyes with a handkerchief. For months Pa had refused to be transferred to a small, backward inland city to help start a new mining machinery factory there. Now he had no choice but to volunteer for the transfer. He wanted to give his unworthy son a fresh start over a thousand miles away from where he had disgraced himself.

"Teacher Yu?" the principal puzzled slightly and looked up from his executive desk in his spacious corner office on the sixth floor of the new Central Building. A man in his mid-40s, a sparkly red-patterned tie on a white dress shirt, the principal looked energetic, confident, and scholarly. He stood up to shake my hand warmly.

"Jiye Yu," I said and explained briefly why I was visiting.

"Old Yu came back for a reunion a couple of years ago, in 1998. Just a second." The principal sat down in his leather armchair and typed on the keyboard. "Here it is," he announced after clicking the mouse a few times and scrolling to the bottom of the computer screen. Then he grabbed a slip of paper and jotted down something on it.

About thirty minutes later I was knocking on the door of Apartment 209 of a tall building in a new, Mediterranean-style residential complex.

A fortyish woman opened the door.

"You're looking for. . .?"

"Teacher Yu. You are. . .?"

"I'm Mrs. Yu. Come in."

Mrs. Yu? Teacher Yu's wife, the woman who had come to the school with a bundle of clothing 30 years ago, must be in her 60's now. The woman in front of me was. . . . Somehow, she looked familiar, as if I had seen her or known her in another life of mine. There was something about her face. She sounded faintly familiar, too.

I told Mrs. Yu that I was a pupil of her husband's many, many years ago and the author of a big-character poster that—

"Oh, you *are*!" Mrs. Yu blurted out my name, giggled like a school girl, and blushed. Her eyes sparkled with hearty joy.

"Ah? You're Meiling! Meiling Wang?" I stammered, feeling my face reddening.

"Yes!" Meiling giggled a bit more, then became the more appropriate Mrs. Yu again.

No, she didn't look like the little Meiling I had remembered and dreamed of every now and then all these years. She was taller, and much more plump. Even the light makeup she had on couldn't completely shield the marks left by the passage of time. Yet her eyes, her nose, and that small birthmark above her right upper lip hadn't changed. She was still the same Meiling. But Meiling, Mrs. Yu?

Mrs. Yu handed me a bottle of chilled mineral water from the refrigerator and told me what happened after my family moved away.

Teacher Yu remained in solitary confinement for two months without putting one word on the stack of papers on the table in that small room in the back of the school yard. He was expelled from the school and arrested on the same day. His crimes? Corrupting the young minds with feudal, bourgeois weeds. Ghostwriting an explosive reactionary and anti-Party big-character poster. Being mulish in his refusal to repent. And living a decadent, bourgeois lifestyle—the irrefutable, in-your-face evidence was his head of fluffy hair combed all the way to the back. It was the saddest day for Meiling, Taozi, and everyone else in my class when they saw their beloved teacher, handcuffed, hair like a sparrow's nest being turned inside out, being taken away in a Beijing jeep after a loud Anti-Jiye Yu Rally.

Mrs. Yu sniffled. Her eyes glistened with moisture. I felt a lump in my throat, too.

"What happened after that?" I ventured after a prolonged pause. "I mean, how did you—"

"Become Mrs. Yu?" She smiled shyly and turned her eyes outside the floor-length window.

Meiling Wang didn't see Teacher Yu again until 1994 at a market for temporary help. She had lost her husband to a boiler explosion and her job at an appliance factory to foreign competition. Teacher Yu had stayed in jail for two years when a major shift in the government policies occurred. While in jail, his wife, a dancer with the Municipal Art Troupe, had divorced him and taken their two small children. A year after he was released, Teacher Yu was assigned a teaching position at a faraway, rural middle school. He had lived there in a small thatched hut for almost ten years when his old employer invited him back to make right the wrong it had done him in the past and to strengthen its language curriculum. Another ten years later, when Teacher Yu finally retired, he found himself still alone, in poor health, and in dire need of someone taking care of most of the domestic chores.

"Two years later," Mrs. Yu murmured, blushing again, "We were together. It was fate. I mean the day we got married, it was so like a dream."

Mrs. Yu stood up and showed me around their simple, but tastefully decorated two-bedroom apartment. The walls in Teacher Yu's study were lined floor to ceiling with bookcases bursting with *Complete Tang Poetry, Dream of the Red Chamber, War and Peace, The Starry Messenger*, and other such books. My heart skipped a beat when I spotted something familiar in the corner of one bookcase with glass doors: a pocket-sized little book with scarlet red plastic wrap.

Mrs. Yu didn't want to tell me where her husband was at that moment and what he was doing. "You'll find out," she flashed me a mysterious smile.

"By the way," I asked as we sat down in the back of a taxi. "Do you still remember Taozi? Taozi Guo?"

"Taozi? Of course!" Mrs. Yu enthused. "He's a professor of classic Chinese literature at Nanjing Normal University. Quite a Tang poetry expert. He comes to visit at least once a year. Teacher Yu is most proud of him. Oh, he'll be so happy to see you, too, after so many years!"

We remained quiet as the taxi neared a huge construction site crammed with giraffe-like cranes, deep-breathing heavy machinery, and laborers in helmets and sweat-soaked shirts. The sun-flooded air quivered with excitement, dust, and thick, bluish smoke. Another colossal shopping center, a cluster of high-rise office buildings, or new European-style residential complex being built here? I wondered.

The taxi driver mumbled a complaint as the car bumped along a narrow, dusty path to the other side of the construction site. Separated from whatever was being built by a tall bamboo fence were more than a dozen low, small sheds of bricks and asphalt felts. I figured that many of the laborers, mostly migrant workers from poor, rural areas of less developed inland provinces, would find shelter in these makeshift homes at the end of their long workday on the construction site. Outside these sheds I could see signs of hurried life: red, pink, and yellow plastic baskets, buckets, basins, tables, and stools.

As Mrs. Yu led me toward a hut near the other end of the

narrow, dusty alley, I picked up a chorus of kids reading aloud. Then I heard a familiar voice explaining something and the kids bursting into a jovial laugh.

Now Meiling and I stood outside a shed not much bigger than the one I had in the backyard of my home in Westchester, NY, and much shabbier. Its door was open. Through it and the glassless windows—big holes in the wall, actually—I could see two dozen or so eight to ten-year-olds sitting upright at small, and semi-crippled desks with books in their hands. Their simple, faded clothing, their sun-baked faces and arms, and the innocent look in their eyes sparkling with eagerness, gave their rustic origin away. The sons and daughters of those migrant workers toiling and sweating on the construction site nearby were so absorbed in what the old man in front of them was saying that they were completely unaware of being observed.

The old man's back humped noticeably. The lines in his face looked deeper in the ardent late afternoon sunlight slanted in through the windows. The book in his left hand quivered. But his voice was still so pleasant, so lute-like. His hair. There was not much hair left on his head now. Whatever hair—all shiny silver—was still on his head was combed neatly all the way to the back.

A small wooden sign in a familiar, elegant handwriting was hanging from a nail near the door of the shed:

Jiye Hope School

Teacher Yu chuckled mirthfully as he continued to explain something to his pupils. Suddenly he became aware of us looking in from outside, turned, nodded, and went on with his class.

I stole a glance at Mrs. Yu. There was such pure reverie in her eyes as she gazed into the shed, her lips half open.

"Now," Teacher Yu said, "Let's read Tu Fu's poem together once again:

In the eighth month autumn's high winds angrily howl—

The sun-dyed air in the dusty alley began to ring with a high-pitched chorus which echoed in the sky above the make-shift sheds and far, far beyond:

In the eighth month autumn's high winds angrily howl
And sweep three layers of thatch from off my house.
The straw flies over the river, where it scatters,
Some is caught and hangs high up in the treetops,
Some floats down and sinks into the ditch.

My eyes misting, I stole another glance at Meiling and both of us joined in the chorus.

Acknowledgements

Heart-felt thanks goes to friends who have inspired me in so many ways: Ed Hagan, for having dared me into fictional ventures; John Briggs, Pat Dickinson, Opal Romano, Karen Jambeck, Yuan Mei-Ratliff, and Alice Zhang, for telling me they liked the first stories I wrote; and Oscar De Los Santos, Kelly Goodridge, JJ Sargent, and Emily Olson, my fellow "Writing Wackos," for countless fun evenings enjoying and critiquing one another's stories.

Once again I am deeply grateful to Chris Robyn at Long River Press for his intelligent guidance and thoughtful work all the way.

Finally, this book is for my father who suffered horrendously during the Cultural Revolution. I owe so much to my father and mother for their love, and to Xiaohong, and Frank, for their loving support.

A native of China, Shouhua Qi came to the United States in 1989. His writings have appeared in *Feminist Studies, AMBIT, The Connecticut Review, Rain Flower,* and many other publications. He is Associate Professor of English at Western Connecticut State University, and the author of *When the Purple Mountain Burns: A Novel; Bridging the Pacific: Searching for Cross-Cultural Understanding Between the United States and China,* and more than ten other books.